One was black and the other was white and they had switched!

After witnessing a violent quarrel between his parents, Greg feels confused, resentful and angry. His father accused his mother of having an affair fifteen years ago, and if the details of the affair are true, then the man that Greg had always called father is not his real father. Even worse is the fact that after striking his mother, Greg's "father" walks out. Meanwhile, Greg has only his mother's word that his father is really his father.

Into this mix comes the **link.**

Steve hates his stepfather. He has struggled for years to find out why his mother would choose to remain with a man who physically abuses her. Steve's secret fear is that his stepfather is actually his real father. Frustrated and angry, Steve goes for his stepfather's gun.

And then there is the **link**.

Neither boy is able to deal with his family's problems; each needs help. And suddenly, help is available! They switched! Greg is now faced with Steve's family's problems and Steve has Greg's. But that's not all. Suddenly, family matters are no longer the biggest problem. Because Greg is black and Steve is white, each boy now faces the question of race from a different perspective. Fearful that no one will believe the switch-- and even more fearful of becoming experimental subjects-- they struggle on their own to survive. They are forced to share information, communicate and–even worse in their eyes–get along with each other.

Demarche Publishing LLC

P.O. Box 36
Mohegan Lake, NY 10547
http://www.demarchepublishing.com

Linked

PRINTING HISTORY
Demarche Publishing LLC/ May 2009

For purchase information contact:
Demarche Publishing LLC
P.O. Box 36
Mohegan Lake NY 10547

Library of Congress Control Number: 2009923682

ISBN: 978-0-9823077-0-0
Printed in the United States of America

To my son George who hates taking
pictures but managed with
the help of his friend Matt.
Thanks Matt!

Linked

Olive Peart

Demarche Publishing LLC

Chapter One

His heart was pounding as he watched the weapon. It glittered in the glare of the fluorescent light. It wasn't a knife, but the threat was real. Calm down. Calm down. He tried reassuring himself. It's only a letter opener. No way! Daniel would never kill us.

But the man wielding the letter opener was livid! "I won't have it! Do you hear me? I won't have it!"

The fury in those words made him cringe, especially since it was emphasized with a stabbing motion that drove the letter opener into the desk.

Then, with a quick motion, the man released the weapon and moved toward them. They retreated in panic.

"Daniel, please," his mother was begging, again. But she knew pleading with her husband was useless. He too knew it was useless. A spurt of anger overcame his fear

"Mom!" He was frantic as he tried to get her out of harm's way—to shield her. But he was too slow, way too slow. A backhanded blow caught her across the face. She stumbled into him and he awkwardly supported her weight.

"Leave her alone! Leave her alone!" he screamed as he tried to drag his mother behind him. But she was resisting. Trying to protect him!

"Steve!" she cried out.

But it made no difference. The man was on her in a flash, striking at her again.

* * * *

Shit! Greg's eyes flew open. He sat up with a jerky gasp and looked around wildly. The streetlight dimly illuminated the room and as he picked out familiar objects he slowly relaxed.

With a deep sigh of relief he collapsed back on the pillow. *Oh Crap!* There was no man... no attack. He was home; his mother was safe. Greg rested his hands over his heart—in reassurance and to calm its erratic beat. It was just a dream. No, a nightmare! And it seemed unbelievably real. He took some deep breaths then rolled over. Automatically, he glanced at Germain's bed, then paused. The lump on the bed did not look real. Why would Germain be bundled under so many covers in mid May? Greg got up and slowly padded over to the next bed, his nightmare forgotten. He clenched his fist as he stared in fury at the empty bed. How could Germain? He had given his word...!

Greg paced back and forth a few times, trying to concentrate. The result was scattered fragments of nothing, plus disturbing remnants of the nightmare. With a groan of disgust he gave up.

The room wasn't made for pacing anyway—what with two beds, two dressers, and too much junk. Germain collected everything, and he kept his stuff in piles of assorted boxes beside, under and around his bed. Greg didn't know how he kept track of the different piles. There were boxes of stones, pens, stamps and coins. You name it, Germain collected it.

Greg was the total opposite. Anything that couldn't fit into his dresser or under his bed was thrown out. There was a straight imaginary line dividing the room that even Germain respected. Any junk that crossed the line was dumped.

After a bit he took a peek out the third-floor apartment's window that overlooked the street. Not much activity, which was normal; this was Paigeton, not the city. He glanced at his bedside clock radio. Twelve o'clock. It didn't even make sense to try to find Germain. Greg had no idea what time Germain had left. He frowned. Something was wrong.

Suddenly it hit him. He was no longer mentally linked with his dad! For a minute, a feeling of panic threatened to overwhelm him. Something was wrong. Did that mean...? He hated to imagine the worst. But what if his dad was dead?

Greg sank down on the side of the bed. Much as he hated his dad, he did not want him dead! Bending forward, he covered his face in his hands. *Shit!* It was a strange feeling—not having the link. He couldn't read minds or anything, but throughout his life he had been aware of a mental link—a sort of emotional awareness—between him and his father. But now he felt nothing. His thoughts were blank. No.... Not blank; simmering in the background, just waiting to come out, was the nightmare. *No!* He didn't want to think about that now.

Greg blinked back tears. His link was gone. He had expected it to go, just as his dad was gone. But still... as long as he had the link there had been a deep-seated hope that things would work out. After all, his reasoning went, how could he be linked mentally with someone who was not a part of his life? But now even that hope was gone. As he dashed a hand across his face, he realized how pointless it was to think about it. There was nothing he could do.

Damn Germain! He did not doubt that Germain had gone to visit his father. He tried unsuccessfully to repress his immediate and intense feeling of betrayal. *How could he? Again! And what if Mom found out? How could Germain do this to her?*

Greg turned and pummeled his pillow for a few mindless seconds. *Damn! Damn! Damn!* He finally collapsed on the bed, mentally if not physically exhausted. He would never again cry over that man. Never! After a few calming breaths, he sniffed. *What should he do now?* No sensible plan came to mind. Greg stretched out on his bed again. He would try to stay up....

About an hour later, Germain slipped quietly into the room.

Greg watched in silence as his brother quickly removed his shoes and shirt and continued his preparations for bed. "That was some promise you made, huh? And fool that I was, I believed you."

Germain jerked around, startled. "Mind your own business," he muttered.

"This is my business." Of necessity Greg's voice was low, but his intense feeling of frustration was clear. "How could you? Hell! After what he did? And we agreed we would never see him, no matter what. You promised!"

"YOU promised," Germain retorted.

"You agreed with me." Greg could not believe what he was hearing.

"Shut the hell up!" Germain's voice had risen. He now sat on the bed and made a visible effort at control. He lowered his voice and continued. "Look, Greg. You're only looking at one side. You could never see his side. Will you just listen...?"

"Listen! You retard! Did you forget that we were listening while he beat our Mom?"

"Damn it, Greg. He had a reason...."

"Yes! He's a vicious bastard! Hell, Germain! How can you defend him after what he did? I don't believe I'm hearing this. How could you?"

"He's my father!" Germain said violently.

There was total silence.

It was a low blow. A cruel, low blow and Greg had no comeback; it was the truth. Nine months ago—after a violent quarrel between his mother and the man he had called Dad all his life—he had learned the truth. Dad was not his father. Worse, he did not even know who his father was. His mother refused to talk. And Dad had walked out after striking his mother. No explanations. Nothing. The entire evening was still engraved in Greg's mind.

* * * *

It happened in mid-August. One evening their father was late picking them up from camp. Greg had been feeling uneasy all evening. Something was not right—but what? Because of the mind link he knew that his father was physically okay. But Greg knew something was wrong.

"What's up Dad?" Greg asked, as soon as he got into the car.

His father refused to make eye contact. "Nothing."

This was bad, Greg thought uneasily. *Real bad.* Greg wished he could read minds. But this link was not like that. Although Greg could always accurately sense feelings, he was never sure about events. When he was about five or six, and first became aware of the link, he used to believe his father was linked to him too. Now he was sure that it was a one-way link; his father had never indicated that he was aware of it.

Greg shot his brother a disturbed look.

Germain just shrugged.

That meant nothing. He and Germain were not always on the best of terms and Germain would sometimes act casual just to annoy him, especially when Germain knew he was upset.

The journey home was completed in silence. Greg turned to stare out the window. He was only vaguely aware as the car turned onto their street. He hugged his body as a horrible feeling of dread engulfed him. The silence remained unbroken as their father parked the car in the underground parking and they took the elevator up to their apartment.

Mom was home.

"Hi, darlings." She came toward them with a warm smile.

Without greeting her or saying a word, their father stalked toward the master bedroom.

She gave Germain and Greg a puzzled glance, looking a little hurt.

Greg instinctively moved closer to her to comfort her. He loved his dad; he was mentally linked with his dad, but he still felt extraordinarily close to his mother. He sometimes wondered if he hadn't deliberately cultivated the closeness because of the strange link he had with his dad. "We don't know what's wrong."

She gave him a distracted look before absently brushing away his arms and following her husband into the bedroom.

The door closed.

Greg and Germain stood outside the door and tried to listen. Their parents had a normal marriage, and they had their share of quarrels. But they always made up afterwards. Both boys expected the same results today. They were intensely curious, however.

But the quarrel taking place in the bedroom started as a low, indistinct rumble. At first their mother sounded pacifying—her tone a sharp contrast to the violent fury in her husband's voice. Gradually, however, her anger increased. The voices became louder, more strident.

"The truth! The truth! What the hell do you know about the truth?"

"Guy, please...."

"You just admitted you knew him. Damn you!"

"He was a friend. Just a friend. I've never...."

"Shut up!"

"Guy...."

A distinct sound followed—flesh striking flesh. Greg drew back in alarm and then started for the door as he heard his mother scream. A loud crash followed.

By this time Greg's hand was on the doorknob. He did not get a chance to turn the knob. The door flew open. The furious man standing there was barely recognizable as his father.

"Get the hell out of my way!"

Greg moved automatically, too shocked to do anything else.

His father dragged two suitcases out of the room. As he approached the door, he turned to point a furious finger at Greg. "You'd better tell her not to try getting child support for you. I have one son, and that's Germain. You heard me, boy? I have one son." He slammed the door as he barreled out of the apartment.

Greg could only stare after him in shock. Then he heard his mother's quiet sobs. He took a quivering breath and rushed into the bedroom. His mother was on the floor, weeping and holding her face. His father had hit her. It was obvious. Her face was already puffy from the blow. She had fallen, taking a standing lamp with her. As Greg hurried to her side, he tried to blank out what he had just heard, but the horror of his father's words was already beginning to overwhelm him.

"Mom! Mom! Are you alright?"

"Yes. Yes." She stared tearfully up at him. "Oh Greg. Oh Greg."

"He left," Greg stated unnecessarily, as he struggled to understand. Only by clamping down on his emotions could he refrain from breaking down completely. That would not help his mother now. He had to stay calm. His father worked as a computer specialist on a cruise ship and was at sea for about half the year. In general, he was away up to eight weeks at a time, which meant that they were often on their own. As the eldest, Germain should have been the one to shoulder major responsibilities, but somehow it had always been Greg who took charge.

Now his mother allowed him to help her to her feet. He slowly guided her to the bed. She was still crying and holding her face. What should he do? Greg looked up. Germain was still standing at the door. His face mirrored the shock Greg was feeling.

Greg sat on the bed with her. Germain slowly entered the room and sat at her other side. He awkwardly patted her on her back as Greg hugged her close. Neither boy said anything. After what seemed like hours but was in reality only a few minutes, her sobs diminished, then finally stopped. She took a few shuddering breaths.

"Did he really leave?"

"Yes," Greg muttered. It was a shock seeing his mother in this condition.

She got slowly to her feet. They sat helplessly, watching as she walked to the window and stared out.

"He's your father," she finally said after a long silence. "Don't worry, Greg. He's your father. A paternity test will prove it."

Galvanized into action by her words, Greg jumped to his feet. "I don't want him as my father," he said furiously. "And I'm not going to give any blood to prove he is. Not after what he did to you."

"He was just angry," Germain began.

"He had no right hitting her," Greg interrupted. "How can you defend him?"

Germain gave a nervous laugh. "Come on, Greg. He's our father."

"No." Greg backed away. "He's YOUR father. Not mine. He's NOT my father."

"Greg!" his mother pleaded.

But he didn't want to hear. Suddenly it was just too much. He backed out of the room and then ran out of the apartment. Too furious and hurt to wait for the elevator, he took the stairs two at a time. And he was still running when he left the apartment building. He had no idea where he was going, or what he hoped to prove. The only plan was to get away, as fast and as far as he could.

A painful cramp in his side finally forced him to stop. Greg collapsed on the ground, panting and crying. It was now dark. Slowly, painfully, he got up. What should he do now? The last thing he wanted to do was go home—not right yet. After some deep breaths, he began walking—aimlessly. Since he was still linked to the man he used to call Dad, he was battling both his anger and his father's. Ruthlessly, he suppressed the link- deliberately focusing on his own emotions. It was like trying to blank out a tune that was stuck in memory but enough was enough. Right now he wanted nothing to do with that man.

Shortly after ten—he had been wandering for more than two hours—a police cruiser pulled up beside him. Until it stopped, Greg didn't even notice it, he was so deep in unwanted thoughts. Startled, he turned to run.

"Hold it! Stop right there!" a voice called out.

How many times had he been warned: never run from the police? Yet, instinctively, he did. And he would have gotten away, too, if he hadn't run up a dead end. Well, he should have known better. Many of these residential streets were dead ends. Greg turned, but before he could assess his situation he was brought down by a flying tackle. Once he was down, the questions began. When he remained silent the officer soon became annoyed, threatening to take him in because he was underage. Finally, after ordering him to stay still, the officer backed away and radioed in.

Greg was numb. He had stopped struggling as soon as he realized he could not escape. Now he just waited. He felt nothing, not even fear.

Later, at the police station, he continued his silence refusing to answer any questions. Although they could not charge him with any crime, as a juvenile he could be released only to an adult. They could only guess at his age, but Greg knew that he looked even younger than his fifteen years. They finally gave up, and would have locked him up for the night if his mother hadn't appeared. Fortunately for him, she had reported him missing and was therefore called in to identify a youth fitting his description.

She was furious. Greg didn't blame her, but he really didn't care. He silently listened to her lecture. Since he was incapable of dealing with it, he simply blanked it out. *Tomorrow. Maybe tomorrow something will change.*

* * * *

Nothing changed the next day or the next month. In the intervening nine months things had gotten worse, not better. His mother had twice tried to get him to a clinic for blood testing. Since Greg knew that the whole point of the exercise was to do a paternity test, he had refused each time. He had threatened to run away if she forced the issue. So far she had not pushed it and Greg wasn't sure what he would do if she insisted. He did not want to have anything to do with *That Man.*

That was not the worst of his worries. A month after the breakup, through a lawyer, his father had demanded that he be allowed to have visitation rights—with Germain only. It was agreed that Germain would visit him every other weekend. However, Greg and Germain both decided never to see their father. With him away on the ship, keeping the promise had been easy so far. Then, two months ago, their father returned and Greg discovered that Germain was seeing him secretly. After a major blow up—fortunately not witnessed by their mother—Greg had extracted Germain's promise not to do so again. But now—now he had just discovered that Germain's promises were worthless.

Greg didn't even try to break the silence. On one level he even understood Germain's frustration and the need to see their father. *It's worse for me.* Technically, he had no father! There were times over the past few months when he'd been rational enough to realize that he was drowning himself in self-pity. Unfortunately, those times were few and far between; most of the time he just felt mad. He felt he had to do something, anything—just to get even. Never mind that he was mostly hurting himself! He hated *That Man.* And the conflicting fury and anger he was still occasionally picking up in the link, whenever he lowered his guard, definitely did not help.

Greg turned over and pretended to sleep. He was beginning to hate Germain, too, because Germain was starting to blame their mother for the breakup of the family—also, because Germain was secretly seeing his father.

Both Greg and Germain had trouble getting up the next morning. He sleepily turned off his alarm when the noise blared and didn't blink again until his mother's shouts woke him up.

"Germain! Greg! It's past six. You know you have to get out by quarter-past-seven. Come on! I shouldn't have to wake you up. What did I give you alarms for?"

"I'm awake. I'm awake," Germain grumbled, as he slid out of bed. "Greg is the one still sleeping."

Greg gave Germain a hard glare before leaping out of bed. He made a dash for the door, but Germain tackled him just as he reached it. Thump! They crashed to the floor. Although Greg was taller, Germain was heavier; Greg knew from past encounters, that keeping Germain down would be hopeless. Nevertheless, he tried.

"Let go. You weren't even thinking about the bathroom until I got up."

"Germain! Greg! Stop it!" Their mother had opened the door. "I don't believe this. It's getting late, and you two are fighting. Over what?"

"Greg knew I was going straight into the bathroom and he tried to beat me to it," Germain began.

"I don't want to hear this," their mother interrupted. "Germain! You go first since Greg went first yesterday." She didn't add that since Greg generally woke as soon as his alarm rang, he almost always went first.

Germain gave Greg a triumphant stare as he made his way to the bathroom. Greg scowled but said nothing— he knew he would now be late for school. Whether deliberately or not, Germain always spent a good forty-five minutes in the bathroom.

"You should get up earlier." His mother was not sympathetic, although she, too, was well aware of Germain's habit. No degree of cajoling, threats or punishments had ever got Germain out of the bathroom quicker.

Greg turned away—annoyed. He hated getting to school late!

"What were you and Germain arguing about late last night?"

Her question got Greg's prompt attention. "You heard?"

His mother shrugged. "Something woke me up." She ran a harried hand through her short black hair. She had only just taken the rollers out, so her action merely increased the confused tumble of curls. "I heard the murmuring."

Greg glanced in the direction of the bathroom. The door was closed. "Uh, nothing."

His mother stared in silence. Greg lowered his head and scuffed at the carpet with a bare toe.

Finally, she sighed. "Okay, Greg. I hope you would let me know if it was important."

"Sure, Mom," Greg said, with an uncomfortable shift, not quite able to meet her eyes.

Not surprisingly, she didn't appear to believe him. She sighed again. "I don't know why the two of you can't get along...."

Greg didn't bother answering that one. *Parents!* As far as he was concerned, he and Germain got along fabulously, considering.... Besides, Greg knew that she knew exactly why he and Germain were hardly talking. Before the big quarrel, Germain had resented him. He mentally checked off the reasons. He got good grades effortlessly, while Germain generally ended up failing. Germain got held back, so now they were both in the same grade, although he was a year-and-a-half younger. And Germain felt that their mother loved Greg best. A big lie, as far as Greg was concerned. He felt his mother often bent over backwards to be fair to Germain. Since the quarrel, the resentment on Germain's side was worse, since Germain blamed him and his mother for the breakup. On his side.... Greg turned away. It really wasn't worth going there....

His life was spiraling hopelessly out of control. He couldn't seem to work up the effort to make the necessary changes. In fact, his behavior was deliberately complicating his life.

Greg spent some—if not all—of the first period in absentminded distraction. He was bored. Not that he missed much of the lecture. He had a phenomenal short-term memory and could play back virtually an entire lecture session in his head. He quickly packed up his workbook to head for the next class. Mr. Stevens, his biology teacher, called to him.

"Greg!"

Greg hesitated but did not turn around. "I'll be late for my next class." The last thing he wanted was a discussion of his class grades. He knew Mr. Stevens was disappointed in his work this school year.

"Two minutes. I'll follow you to the next class."

Greg reluctantly turned. Mr. Stevens matched his pace as they walked along the corridor.

"You know, Greg. I've never come across someone like you before. After our last talk, when was it—four, five months ago?--you've really surprised me."

Greg stared at the ground.

"I guess you have finally perfected your technique."

"I don't know what you're talking about," Greg

muttered.

"No?" Mr. Stevens feigned a look of surprise. "Your grades were astounding last school year but surprise, surprise this year you have had a disastrous start. If you remember, last time we met with your mother about your grades. You were failing, or your grades were fluctuating wildly."

"They are much better now," Greg protested.

"I know." The teacher sounded almost amused. "I've checked with all your teachers. Straight C's. Even on class tests. That must take some effort. What do you do? Calculate how many questions you should answer before each test?"

He was close. Greg cleared his throat. In fact, that was one of the few challenges he still allowed himself.

"Just enough to get by," Mr. Stevens mused. "Just enough not to cause any more alarm, like us contacting your mother again."

"Listen," Greg interrupted, "I really have to go." He didn't want to hear the spiel again—how he was wasting his life. His life was now. And surviving meant getting from day to day without going crazy. Coping with a heavy workload now was out of the question. He was too frustrated and too angry. Why couldn't everyone just leave him alone?

That was why he had deliberately improved his grades. After his first precipitous drop in grades, his mother had told the teachers about the separation and pending divorce but not the reason behind it. He was forced to get counseling and he had hated it. No way did he want anyone prying in his private life. As far as he was concerned, the counseling had turned out to be a waste of time. He had refused to cooperate.

"I want to see you after school," Mr. Stevens insisted.

Greg's jaws clenched.

"It's that or I call your mother again."

Greg acknowledged Mr. Steven's ultimatum with a nod. *Just another problem I don't need.*

Greg sighed and turned away. That was when he spotted Ray. Ray was a mixed kid—his mother was Swiss and his father Jamaican. Greg did not know what Ray's problem was, but this past year Ray had definitely been acting weird—worse than him, even. He and Ray had never been friends. Ray had always been a loner. They had first met a year ago in honors history class. Like him, Ray seemed to have had a precipitous drop in grades. They had both been dropped from their honors and AP classes and now both boys had a number of classes together and were slowly inching toward friendship.

Inching was the word to use because half the time Greg wasn't sure he wanted to have anything to do with Ray. Last year, Greg had tended to stay away from him because, well... because! It was hard to buck the trend, and in this school race was a big issue—you stuck to your racial groups—or else.

Greg used to feel he had enough problems—what with dealing with Germain and all—he didn't feel like fighting the unspoken codes of school too. But this year he didn't care whether the other kids accepted him or not. Ray, however, was definitely trouble. He disrupted classes and was always thinking up some wild plan. Greg was listening, and the temptation to follow through on some of the wilder plans was getting too hard to resist.

"What's up, Greg?" Ray had spotted him at the same time.

"Nothin', man. You?" Greg asked as he approached.

"How about a trip to Manhattan?"

"Manhattan?"

"Yeah. After school. I know a place we can see movies for three dollars."

"Well...." It didn't sound like a bad idea to Greg. But he wasn't sure his mother would allow it.

"C'mon, man. My dad isn't home until late tonight and the last thing I want to do is spend the entire evening by myself. I figure we could go and get back by ten, eleven."

Greg felt a stirring of excitement. This might be just what he needed. He wouldn't tell his mom. She would just say no. Greg thought quickly. He could tell her he was spending some time at a friend's house. *Yeah! That was it.* Going straight home was depressing anyway. He would do it!

"Okay. Sounds good. I have to see the bio teacher after school but I'll meet you by the lockers when I can."

As he had expected, Mr. Steven gave him a long spiel about career paths and how messing up your life now can mess up your future. Greg listened in silence. He was aware that Mr. Stevens was putting out an effort for him and he wished he could appreciate the help, but right now he wanted to be left alone. There were better ways of solving his problems, true, but he didn't feel up to trying Mr. Steven's way.

Finally, Greg gave his watch a pointed glance. Mr. Stevens noted his action but would have ignored him if someone hadn't rapped at the door.

"Come in," the teacher called.

It was another teacher. Greg grinned in relief.

"Do you have a minute?" the teacher asked.

"Sure. This is an ongoing problem. I can always get back to it later." Mr. Stevens gave Greg another warning look. "You can go now, Greg, but just remember what I said. I'll be watching you."

Greg couldn't get out fast enough.

Chapter Two

They left the school grounds cautiously. Greg's heart was racing with excitement. He felt curiously free. He had left a message on the answering machine for his mother.

First they had to take a bus to the train station at White Plains, and there they caught the train to Manhattan. It was great. It was easy. They fooled around for a while, harassing shoppers, messing up store displays and generally creating a nuisance of themselves. For the first time in months, Greg was happy. *This is fun*, he thought as they raced wildly out of a department store.

"Did you see his face?" Ray shouted as they collapsed on each other, laughing hilariously. They had deliberately opened a can of shaving cream and sprayed it on one of the customers.

Greg held his side. "He wanted to sh-shout but couldn't because of the cream in his mouth!" He could hardly get the words out because of his laughter.

Ray sank to the ground. "And the manager. Holy shit!"

It was a while before they could think rationally. Then Greg looked at his watch. "We're going to miss the movie."

"Damn it!" Ray scrambled to his feet.

They had to rush and they still missed a good third of the movie. That was the excuse they gave themselves for staying for the later one. They had to see at least one entire movie! It was close to eleven when they left the movies and began the long walk back to the train station.

Deeply engrossed in reliving each scene of the movie, neither of them was paying much attention to the street around them.

"Got any change?"

Greg was startled by the sudden appearance of a guy, right beside him.

"Change?"

"No," Ray said abruptly.

Oh no! Greg warily took a hasty look at the scene. Four youths were close behind them. He heart began thumping erratically as he realized that the youths were slowly inching forward, trying to surround them.

Using his backpack as a weapon, Greg smacked it into the face of the closest youth. "Run!" he screamed.

His loud shout, and action, gave Ray the necessary diversion. Ray took off. Greg was right behind him but he had gotten off to a slow start. One of the youths thudded into him and sent him sprawling. Greg quickly scrambled to his feet, but he was now surrounded. That's when he realized they were armed with baseball bats. And they were angry. One also had a box cutter. *Not good!*

"The bro thinks he's bad, huh?" one youth taunted him.

Greg was silent. He turned slowly as they circled him. *They wouldn't kill me, would they? Not here.* He tried to control his panic. *What should I do? What can I do?*

"Yeah, he needs a lesson." This from the tallest guy in the group—the obvious leader.

"Yeah, we'll give him one he ain't likely to forget." Suiting actions to words, the youth came in swinging his bat.

Greg brought his bag around to shield his face. The bat smashed into his bag. He stumbled, and backed up to keep his balance. The next blow smashed into his forearm.

"Ow!" Greg cried out. His entire left arm went numb.

He stumbled again and his backpack slipped. Swish! The bat connected solidly with his head. He sank to the ground in a daze, and cried out again as pain began shooting up his arm. Then someone kicked him squarely in his ribs. Greg tried to roll. *Shit!* He felt a stinging sensation on his face. They were slicing him to bits! Unable to see, too dazed to even cry out, Greg curled into a ball and wished for death—a quick death—anything to stop the pain.

* * * *

Greg never heard the sirens of the police patrol car. He later learned that Ray had run no further than the next block, where he had stopped and called first his father and then the police. And the arrival of the police probably saved his life. They were the ones to call an ambulance. He was semiconscious and unable to answer questions at the hospital but they must have got the necessary information from Ray. Greg woke up later that night to find a nurse hovering over him.

She smiled. "Good. You are back with us. You were

very lucky, you know."

Greg gave her a weak smile. His head was splitting. "My head...." He tried raising his arm but found it unnaturally heavy.

"Take it easy," the nurse said. "You have a cast on."

"What happened?"

"Don't you remember?"

Greg frowned. His head hurt too much to think.

The nurse patted his good arm reassuringly. "Take it easy. You got beat up. I'll give you something for the headache."

She did something. Greg guessed she must have injected some medication into the intravenous line attached to his arm. Whatever she gave him, it was enough to put him to sleep. Only vaguely did he remember waking up a number of times during the night. Each time his mother was present, but if she said anything to him he didn't remember it. When he finally became aware, it was morning and his mother and brother were sitting by the bed.

"Thank God!" his mother cried. Germain was silent as his mom petted and fussed over him.

Greg gave a weak smile but did not try to speak, and a shooting flash of pain stopped his first and only attempt to nod his head in response to her question. His agonized expression of pain threw his mother into a panic.

"Oh my God! Don't move! I'll get the nurse."

Greg was in too much pain to stop her. As soon as she left the room Germain bent forward.

"They took your blood." His voice dripped satisfaction.

Greg closed his eyes. Now he really felt sick.

"Serves you right," Germain was smug. "It was a dumb idea to go to Manhattan anyway. Dad says you are out of control."

At that Greg's eyes flew open. He found his voice. "Dad is here?" he whispered incredulously.

"No. But I called him. I told him everything."

Greg closed his eyes again, furious with himself. *Now they would do a paternity test!* Worse, he had just called the man Dad. He had promised himself he'd never, ever do so again.

"You were lucky your friend was able to call the police," Germain continued in a low voice. "If...." He stopped abruptly as their mother entered the room, with a nurse close behind her.

"He had a mild concussion," the nurse was explaining. "He will have a lot of pain for a few days. That's normal." She turned to Greg. "Did you get any pain medication this morning?"

"I don't think so...." Greg muttered. He didn't want to hear any more. *They took my blood! I hate this!* He stared blankly into space as the nurse checked his medical chart before finally producing two pills for him to swallow.

His mother settled back into the chair by his bed. "Feeling better now?"

He would never feel better! How could she have done this to him?

"When... when will I get to go home?" he asked.

"The doctor should be here sometime today to examine you. He told me he should be able to discharge you this evening." She paused. "What were you doing in

Manhattan?"

"He was playing truant." Germain sounded disgustingly satisfied. "Ever since you and Dad broke up, he's been acting up. I guess this was supposed to be his big rebellion act."

"Greg?" His mother turned to him. She looked pained. "I thought you had more sense, Greg."

Greg turned away and closed his eyes. He wished they would both leave.

"Greg!" Yes, she was definitely angry.

"My head...." he pleaded, only partly faking.

"They batted you in the head," Germain spoke. "They also broke your left arm and you got a broken rib. And they sliced up your face and arms. You got forty stitches. The police stopped them or they would have killed you. Maybe next time you'll come straight home."

"That's enough, Germain," their mother interrupted. "Your brother is not well and you aren't making things any better."

"If I had done that...." Germain began.

"Leave it, Germain. I'll speak to Greg later, when he feels a little better." His mother was still mad, but she finally accepted that he was really too ill to deal with her lecture. "Okay Greg. We'll talk about this when you get home." She stood up. "I have to leave for work now. And Germain, you have to get to school. I'll be back later. I told my boss I would be late but I have to go in. There's an important meeting that I have to attend this afternoon. Will you be okay?"

"Yeah." Greg neither turned around nor opened his eyes.

His mother stood indecisively for a minute then reached down to pat his arm. "Later then. Come on, Germain."

Greg waited until he was sure they had both left the room before turning around. He blinked back tears. He wished he could get out of this family—disappear somehow.

* * * *

Greg spent the day resting. He was happy when he discovered there was really only one bad slice across his face. It started at his ear and ended slightly above his chin, almost following the curve of his jaw. Because of the location, the doctor said the final scar would not be too bad. All the other slices were on his arm, which he had used to protect his face. So he was feeling much better that evening when Ray and Ray's father came in. They were both upset.

"I'm sorry," Ray said. "This is all my fault. You would never have got beat up if I didn't get you involved."

Greg started to protest but Mr. Brent, Ray's father, stopped him. "No, Greg. I've already been through this with Ray. It was his fault. He was wrong. He's been acting up because of problems at home but this should never have happened."

"No one forced me to go," Greg protested.

"Come on, Greg," Mr. Brent challenged. "Would you have thought to go to Manhattan if Ray hadn't suggested it?"

"Maybe not Manhattan. But I could have done worse." It was painful admitting his motives, but Greg found it difficult not to be honest at this point. In fact it was a relief. "It's partly my fault," he insisted.

Mr. Brent folded his arms across his chest and gave Greg a piercing look. "I see."

"But—"Ray began.

"Leave it, Ray," his father advised. He turned to Greg. "Do you want to talk about it sometime?"

Greg's glance slid away. "Well...."

"Never mind," Mr. Brent sighed when Greg paused. "I'd rather have nothing than a series of lies. Save it."

Greg grimaced, but admitted to himself that he probably would have told a series of lies. "Did you say anything to my mother?"

"She wasn't at home when I called. I left a message and I'm going to try to see her this evening."

Greg tried hard to conceal a frown. He wasn't quite successful.

Mr. Brent lifted an inquiring eyebrow. "Well? Is there some other problem?"

"No. No." But Greg wished he could prevent the meeting. He did not want Mr. Brent to know the extent of his family's problems. And his mother may well confess all, especially now that she was so upset.

Again Mr. Brent waved away his reply. "If you are not going to tell me the real reason save yourself the effort. Don't answer."

With a scowl, Greg looked away. Mr. Brent's no-nonsense manner was getting to him.

Ray gave his father a quick glance then changed the topic. They spent the rest of the visit discussing general topics.

When they left, Greg was feeling much better. If things were different, he would have confided his frustrations to Mr. Brent. He found himself liking Ray's father. Still, he felt he had a friend now—Ray. And he now understood why Ray had been acting so disruptive this past year. A year ago Ray's mother had died after a long illness. Like him, Ray was just trying to cope.

* * * *

In the end, the hospital kept him for two days. They wanted to be sure his head was okay. It was a great two-day break because as soon as he got home, his mother began questioning him. Greg was surprised she had held off for so long. But she was still mad with him, and got angrier when he remained defiant about his trip to Manhattan. They ended up shouting and screaming at each other when he accused her of illegally taking his blood. His one good cheer was when Germain too felt the sting of their mother's tongue. *Serves Germain right! Loser! He's acting like a prick. And I got stuck with him as a brother.*

But by nightfall he was no longer grinning. The dream came back.

Chapter Three

He sped along the corridor to the bedroom. "This time I'll kill him," he vowed. No one was following, yet he still took a hasty glance behind as he opened the door and skidded into the bedroom. Slowly, he eased open the nightstand drawer. "Where is it? Where is it?" He was scattering papers in his haste but he didn't care. "Damn it! It has to be here." It was here the last time. But the last time was months ago. It wasn't here now. He straightened up and threw a panicky glance at the door, then ran to the other side of the bed. His search became frantic. At the chest-of-drawers he began opening the drawers and scattering the contents haphazardly on the floor. Just as he moved to the second set of drawers the bedroom door slammed open.

"You bastard! I knew you would run in here."

He jerked upright and began backing away.

"I should have done this years ago." The man was removing his belt.

"No!"

At first he thought he was under attack again. His hands came up to protect his face. But it was impossible to fight back. At six-foot-two he was close to six inches taller than the man but he was slighter, by a good one hundred pounds.

Shit! The pain! A cry almost escaped, but he bit down hard. No tears. No sound. Crying would give this man too much satisfaction. No way would this man make him cry. But the pain!

Greg finally caught on. He was being whipped. It was endless. When it finally stopped, his arms and back were a perpetual mass of pain. A groan did escape then as he curled in a ball. The man muttered something, then finally, finally, he left the room. For a long time Greg just stayed there—too afraid to move. Then he looked down at his arms. *Thank God it isn't yet summer. At least I'll be able to wear long sleeves to hide the welts.* Even as the thought flashed across his mind he jerked. *Shit! This can't be real.* Greg looked down again. His arms were white!

He blinked. And as suddenly as it started, it was gone. The dream was gone. Greg looked around wildly. But he was in bed—in his room. The cast on his arm got in the way, but nevertheless, he hugged his body and began shivering. *Shit! What did this mean?* He squeezed his eyes tightly shut—to block out the vivid images. But even as he did, they invaded his mind. *No, that was no dream! It was real!* He had been in a strange bedroom. A man had whipped him and now he was hurt. Impossible! He opened his eyes again, straining, trying to keep the images. Try as he could, the images slowly lost focus, then faded. It was no good. The dream—the images—whatever it was, was gone. Thinking was impossible. His head was throbbing. Greg sank back on his pillow.

* * * *

"Greg?"

Greg startled, then realized it was Germain. He took a deep breath and relaxed again. "What?"

"If you're in pain, take a pain killer or something. If you keep moaning like that I'll never get any sleep."

Greg hadn't realized he had moaned out loud. He gave a sorry-sounding mumble.

Germain grunted in return. "Just keep quiet."

Greg kept quiet as his mother and brother prepared to leave the apartment. When his mother looked in on him, he assured her he was okay so she would leave quickly. But he still felt sore all over. It was hard for him to tell whether he was affected by his injuries or those of the boy in his dreams—probably both.

After a fitful doze he woke. Someone was gently brushing back his hair. Greg reluctantly opened his eyes expecting to see his mother. But the woman bending over him was a stranger. It was impossible not to stare. She had shoulder-length blond hair—carefully styled and curled. Her face was well dressed with foundation, lipstick, and eye makeup. From this angle, looking up at her, Greg could just make out a skillfully covered bruise on her jaw. He blinked, then looked around cautiously, expecting the vision to disappear. But no.... She was real! And so was the room. It definitely was not his room. This room was large, with a wide screen TV and a huge queen-size bed plus matching student desks and dressers. Then there was the computer. Wow! There was even a massive walk-in closet. It covered one entire wall. And from the window on the other side of the room he could see trees—just trees and more trees. Woods! He closed his eyes again. *He had to be dreaming*!

"Steve?" she asked.

Greg could only stare.

"How are you feeling?"

Stunned! Shocked! He didn't say anything, however. He was still trying to gather his thoughts. He had instantly recognized her as the lady in his earlier dreams. But she thought he was her son! *Is she blind?*

"Steve... Steve? I'm sorry," the lady said. "I never meant for you to get caught up in this mess."

Greg thought of the whipping her son had received last night. What sort of excuse was that? He kept his head turned away, hoping she would leave.

"I have to go now," she finally said.

He still refused to even look at her. He was too scared.

"Steve. Please. I have to go to a meeting." She hesitated. "He left early. He had a board meeting. Steve, please don't do anything rash. Promise me you won't tell."

Greg was silent. He had been shocked into silence after looking down at his arms. *I'm white?* Now he needed time—time to sort things out.

"Steve?" she pleaded.

"Okay," he muttered, after giving her a quick glance—anything to get rid of her quickly. Something was drastically wrong. Maybe if she left, things would get back to normal. *He* would get back to normal!

The lady patted his head again. "Stay in bed, okay. I called the school so there shouldn't be a problem. Just rest up for today." Again she hesitated. "He thought you were trying to find his gun. That's why he got so angry."

At that he turned away again. His thoughts veered

to the whipping. He wasn't yet sure what had happened, but somehow it was him and not her son who had been whipped last night.

"Steve, try to understand. I've explained to you...."

He really didn't want to hear this. No amount of explanation could excuse what that man had done.

Something in his expression must have clearly depicted his thoughts because she stopped and sighed. "I'll be back soon," she paused at the door. "I... I told Laura she could have the rest of the week off so I'm dropping her off at her sister's. But I left some sandwiches in the kitchen. There is also enough junk food around so you really shouldn't be hungry," she added, trying to lighten the mood.

When Greg did not respond she quietly closed the door, and not a minute too soon. He heard a shocked exclamation of horror.

* * * *

Panicky thoughts were mingled with deep confusion. Greg felt as if his head was bursting. "Stop!" he screamed aloud. Silence—a deafening silence. The other boy—and he was sure it was Steve—was still panicky. But Greg's shouted command had calmed him somewhat.

< "What's happening? Where am I?"> The tone was hesitant and uncertain.

< "I don't know how it happened but I think we somehow switched places,"> Greg explained. < "I'm at your house—or my mind is—and you're at mine.">

< "Holy shit! I'm black!"> Steve sounded horrified.

Greg suddenly laughed. Now that he came to think about it, this was funny. He always wondered what it would be like to be white!

< "Will you shut up and think of a way to switch us back?"> Steve was furious.

< "Alright,"> Greg agreed, in between laughs.

< "This is serious!"> Steve shouted. < "I don't want to be black!">

< "I hear you. You don't have to shout. You don't even have to talk out loud. I can hear you mentally.">

< "Can you hear me now?"> Steve asked mentally.

< "Yup,"> Greg said. Then there was a silence. < "Steve?">

< "Hah! So you can't hear everything.">

< "What do you mean?">

< "I was thinking some other things and you didn't hear. Did you?">

< "No.... "> Greg agreed slowly. He was thinking about last night. < "Steve, what happened last night? Were you whipped or was I?">

< "I remember the start of the whipping. But I think.... I thought.... I passed out or something. I don't remember anything else until this morning.">

< "Well, I remember,"> Greg said flatly. < "I was whipped. I remember looking down at my arms. For a minute I was white, then it disappeared.">

< "We must have switched for a few minutes last night,"> Steve admitted.

< "Long enough for me to get your whipping,"> Greg accused.

< "Yeah? Well, what about when you got beat up?">

< "You were there?">

< "My mother thought I was sick or something. I

doubled up moaning just as I was going up to bed. I was just lucky it didn't last long."»

Greg was silent, thinking. *That could be why I am alive—because you took some of my beating.*

‹ "You bet that's why,"› Steve agreed instantly.

Greg started. ‹ "You heard that?"›

‹ "I sure did."› Steve sounded smug. ‹ "You aren't blocking your thoughts. I can just about read your mind."›

Greg concentrated. ‹ "Bet you can't read it now."›

‹ "No."› Steve admitted.

‹ "I think I have this figured out,"› Greg relaxed again. With a little concentration he found that he could block most of his thoughts from Steve, while projecting only what he wanted Steve to hear. ‹ "I started having dreams about you just four or five days ago. How about you?"›

‹ "Same here. But mine weren't dreams really. I saw you in the daytime too. Like a daydream. If I stared in space, a picture of you doing something would just pop in my head. I thought I was going crazy or something."›

They spent a few minutes sorting things out and practicing. Finally, after experimenting, they figured that they could project their thoughts as well as the surrounding picture to each other. Greg was able to project mental pictures and sound images of his surroundings. He was able to let Steve hear the radio playing in the room.

Steve, on the other hand, could project only picture images of his surroundings, and he was unable to block Greg's mental images. But Steve could read Greg's mind lots easier. Greg had to actively work to stop Steve from reading his mind. Steve also projected his feelings unconsciously.

If he was angry, Greg was immediately swamped with his anger unless Steve made a conscious effort not to project that anger.

Greg collapsed on the bed. < "My headache is getting worse. Let's get back to the right places and practice later.">

< "How? How do we get back?">

Good question. Greg had no idea. He had just assumed that the switch was temporary. < "Think about your room, and I'll think about mine,"> he suggested.

They tried.

Nothing.

Next they tried thinking about family members. But that didn't work either.

< "This can't be happening to me,"> Steve moaned.

< "Shut up and think harder,"> Greg advised. Now he was really worried. What if Steve's mother returned? And that man—he didn't want the experience of being white in *this* family. He wanted out of here!

After close to an hour of trying, they both lapsed in an exhausted mental silence.

Greg sank back on the pillow with his eyes closed. He had a pounding headache and his brain kept telling him his arm and ribs were broken. Meanwhile, his eyes were sending a completely different message. The conflicting information was just about the last straw. His mind was about ready to shut down.

After a few minutes of silence, he asked. < "Do you have a headache?"> Maybe they shared the same symptoms.

< "It's pounding,"> Steve muttered. < "And I keep forgetting my arm... your arm, is broken.">

< "Don't you feel it?">

< "No. I feel like I was whipped.">

It was weird. They were feeling mostly their original symptoms. < "Don't you make my arm worse.">

< "Oh yeah. So what are you going to do? Beat me up?">

< "Just shut up, man!">

< "Great idea," > Steve said with irritating mockery. < "I think I'll take a nap.">

Greg didn't bother answering. His eyes were already closing, and he immediately fell asleep.

He wasn't sure what woke him, but when he opened his eyes the man was standing over him.

Oh no! Despite his best effort he was unable to sink into and disappear in the bed.

Chapter Four

< "Steve! Steve!"> He screamed mentally.

< "What the hell is wrong with you?"> Steve grumbled. < "I still have a headache.">

< "Think about your home. Think man, think. Your father is here. He's bending over me. I want out of here.">

Greg felt Steve's involuntary shudder. < "Steve!">

Steve's fear was paralyzing—paralyzing for both of them. Greg closed his eyes in dread.

"You may as well open your eyes, Steve," the man said. "I know you're awake."

Greg opened his eyes. The truth was, he was afraid of doing anything else.

< "He's my stepfather,"> Greg heard Steve's mental whisper. < "He beats my mother. He.... I.... I wish I could kill him.">

Greg tried to stare fearlessly at Steve's stepfather but he was quaking. Tiny tremors kept running throughout his body. His fear was such that it took a while for him to realize that this paralyzing fear was not only his own. Steve was projecting his fear. Even the cover was shaking!

Shit! He had to do something. < "Steve. Back out.

I can't think. You're...."\>

Before he could complete the thought, Steve was gone. For one petrifying instant Greg thought he was gone for good. < "Steve!"> He screamed mentally.

< "I'm trying to back out,"> Steve protested. Greg's cry had forged an even greater link between their minds.

Greg closed his eyes as he was again swamped with fear. His eyes flew open, however, as he felt fingers touching his arm. He flinched. At the same time he became aware of Steve's effort to break the mental link between them. This time he let Steve go.

"Listen, Steve," the man was saying. "I'm sorry."

Sorry! Did I hear right? Greg stared.

"I don't think you'll have any permanent scarring."

Was this really Steve's stepfather, bending over him and examining the raised welts on his arms? Something was wrong with this picture.

< "Steve?"> He called cautiously.

Steve was back instantly.

Greg allowed him to see what was happening. < "He's up to something,"> Steve muttered. However, his fear was receding. < "I don't trust him.">

< "What do you call him?"> Greg asked.

< "I would love to just call him Mr. Pierce but he insists that I call him Dad."> Steve's tone projected his hate.

Having finished his examination, Steve's stepdad straightened. "You will have to stay home for a few days. At least until these disappear. How are you feeling?"

"Fine." Greg said without looking directly at the man.

"Good. Good." After rubbing his hands together,

Mr. Pierce took a few turns around the room. "Steve." He cleared his throat. "You are sensible. You realize that you can't say anything about this." He waved his hands in Greg's general direction. "It would only bring heartache to your mother. You are a minor and you might be taken away," he paused. "You understand what I'm saying."

Greg did indeed understand. Steve's stepfather did not want anyone to know that he beat his wife and whipped his son. The last thing Greg wanted to do was keep the whole thing a secret.

< "You must,"> Steve insisted.

< "Are you mad?"> Greg was incredulous. < "After what he did to you?">

"Steve," Mr. Pierce was getting impatient. "I want your word that you'll tell no one."

Greg stared at him, becoming emboldened by his anger. He was damned if he would....

< "Greg you have to.... "> Steve pleaded. < "My mom....">

Greg took a deep breath and lowered his gaze. "Okay," he muttered.

Mr. Pierce actually patted his arm. "Good. Good." That taken care of, he again rubbed his hands together. "You really were foolish to try to find my gun. What did you plan to do—shoot me?" He sounded incredulous. "It's not kept loaded anyway, so finding it would not have done you much good." Mr. Pierce gave a short laugh.

Greg got the impression he just did not believe Steve capable of doing him any harm.

"Well," he said, as he headed back to the door. "I have to get back to work. I only came home to make sure you were okay. See you later."

Not if I can help it, Greg thought resentfully as he watched the man walk out the door. He had forgotten that he had opened his mind to Steve.

< "Greg. Listen,"> Steve pleaded. < "Just follow the rules and do as he says. He can be vicious, I tell you. And I don't want my Mom getting hurt.">

< "So why stay?"> Greg was still incredulous. < "All you and your mom have to do is go to the police.">

< "I.... I can't. He has some sort of hold on her. She doesn't want to tell me but she gets scared if I even mention the police.">

< "So you'd rather kill him?">

Steve sighed. < "I got mad. He was hitting her last night and I just got mad. I was just going to try and scare him. I know I would never really use it.">

< "This the first time he hit you?">

< "It's the first time he used his belt. Usually if I try to stop him hitting my Mom, he will push me out of the way or once he punched me.">

< "You're acting dumb,"> was Greg's opinion.

< "Just leave it,"> Steve stated flatly. < "You don't know everything. Besides, it's my life—my problem.">

< "I still think....">

< "Will you just leave it? Why don't you tell the police that your father beat up your mother?">

< "That's a lie! He did it once. One time only. This isn't the same!">

< "Oh yeah!">

< "Shut up!"> Greg deliberately blocked out Steve.

* * * *

For a while he played around on the computer, and then he lounged in bed and watched the big screen TV in the room. Finally, he decided to find out what he looked like now.

The boy staring back at him from the mirror was totally unfamiliar. He had straight dark blond hair. His eyes were brown, almost the color he expected his skin to be, but his skin was pale—definitely not the type that tanned easily. Greg felt distinctly uneasy as he looked at his arms and face. Living as he did in a mixed neighborhood, it wasn't that he had no contact with whites, but this was different—now he *was* white! The white face staring at him now seemed almost colorless. Shock probably—he thought with grim humor. Still, what he needed was a tan! He grinned suddenly. Next time he'd suggest that to Steve.

The house was massive compared to what he was used to. There were four huge bedrooms on the top floor. A quick peek in the master bedroom showed a king-size bed, separate walk-in closets and a bathroom with separate his and her vanities.

Steve's bedroom also had a bathroom but the other two bedrooms shared a bathroom. Downstairs, he found that his living room at home could easily fit into the entrance hall here. There was another bathroom—without a bath—a huge kitchen, a dining room, another formal dining area and a family room with television, stereo system, and a sectional sofa set.

Upstairs had wall-to-wall carpeting but on this floor only the family room was carpeted. The other rooms had thick expensive looking rugs on hardwood flooring.

He saw stairs leading to the basement but decided against exploring further. Apart from a lingering headache, he was now hungry. And he was picking up some of Steve's uneasiness. After wolfing down the sandwiches Mrs. Pierce had prepared, he wandered back to Steve's—now his—room. His uneasiness increased. What could be happening? Yet he refused to back down. Steve should contact him first.

In the end he did back down. Steve's fear was getting to him—mentally. It was late evening now, and he needed to know what was happening. Besides, he didn't think he would be able to live with himself if Steve got hurt.

< "Steve?">

< "Your mother just came in,"> Steve muttered.

< "She said anything to you?">

< "I got back in bed. I'm pretending I'm sleeping.">

Greg thought a bit. Much as he hated telling a stranger anything about his family, if he and Steve were going to survive without someone dumping them in a loony bin, they would have to exchange information about each other. As quickly as he could, he filled Steve with information about his mother and brother and briefly explained how he came to be in Manhattan the night he got hurt.

< "What about your Dad?"> Steve asked suddenly.

Greg ground his teeth. His control had slipped and Steve was again reading his mind. < "Why don't I just lie back and make you pick me dry?">

Steve gave the mental equivalent of a shrug. < "You are the one sending me all this extra info I didn't ask for.">

Greg's curiosity got the better of him. < "What did

I send you?">

< "I got, 'I wonder if I should tell him about Dad.'">

< "Oh.">

< "Well? So where is your Dad? I already got most of it from you mentally anyway.">

It made sense to tell him but Greg was still reluctant. Keeping firm control of his thoughts, he finally admitted. < "Nine months ago my parents had a fight and my Dad walked out. That's all there is to it.">

< "Yeah,"> Steve sounded amused. < "And that tells me a lot.">

< "So what's so funny?"> Greg refused to add more.

< "I can feel the control you're putting out to stop me from reading your mind,"> Steve laughed. < "Every time you slip I get some more info.">

Greg scowled. It wasn't fair that he couldn't read Steve's mind while Steve could read his. < "You can have your laugh after you tell me about your family.">

He immediately picked up Steve's shift in emotions. It was his turn to taunt. < "What's the matter, Steve?">

< "Oh shut up.">

Greg continued grinning. Now he understood what Steve meant. He could literally feel the effort Steve was making to keep his emotions in check.

< "Alright, c'mon, give!">

Steve reluctantly began telling about his family. Like Greg, he gave only the basic information. He was an only child and had lived all his life in Rivieren, which was about ten miles northwest of where Greg lived. His mother didn't work officially although along with her charity work she seemed to head a million and one committees. His stepfather was a stockbroker.

Greg digested the information. It wasn't much. They would both need to confide a lot more.

< "What happened to your father?">

< "He died of a heart attack when I was about a year old.">

< "Did your stepfather always beat your mother?">

< "When I was about seven, I saw him punch her. After that I.... I just hated him. Usually he leaves her face alone. He punches her on her body. Once he broke her arm. He just twisted it and it snapped."> Steve paused in remembered anger. < "It's only when he gets really mad that he hits her in the face.">

Greg flinched at the intense feelings of hurt Steve was sending. < "But...?"> With a big effort he managed to control his thoughts. Still, he was confused. Steve's family wasn't exactly poor. The whole situation made no sense. < "But why?">

< "I don't know."> There was anguish in Steve's voice.

< "Does anyone else know?">

< "No."> Steve sighed. < "I don't even think Laura knows.">

< "Laura?">

< "Our housekeeper.">

< "But what do you tell people when they see the bruises?">

< "They don't see anything. Mom always hides any bruise. When her arm broke, she told everybody she fell down the stairs. Even my grandparents.">

< "You have grandparents?">

< "Only my dad's parents. My mom's parents are dead.">

< "What about your stepdad's parents?">

Steve was silent for a minute.

< "Steve?">

< "That's something else I don't understand. We never see them. I don't know why.">

< "When did your mother marry him?">

< "Mom married him right after my father died. I wasn't even two. And don't ask me again why she stays with him. I don't know. Mom gets scared whenever I even suggest we leave. She always begs me not to tell anyone he beats her. I just don't know.">

Greg hesitated then asked. < "A few days ago he came after you with a letter opener?">

< "I went into his study—usually the door is locked—but he left it open and I went in. Just to.... I don't know. I guess I was just curious. I was just looking around. He came in and got mad. Then Mom came in and started defending me so he just lit into her.">

It was getting harder to ignore Steve's hurt and anger. < "Steve!"> he protested.

< "You don't know how I hate that man."> Steve admitted flatly.

< "I know!"> Greg practically shouted. < "Will you stop sending me all your emotions?">

There was a few minutes of silence as Steve got control of his emotions. < "You are lucky you have a father,"> he said abruptly.

< "I don't."> Greg was just as abrupt.

< "Huh?">

Greg gave a mental shrug. There really was no point hiding it. Steve would eventually find out anyway. < "He says he isn't my dad and Mom says he is. Personally I don't care.">

< "Yeah, sure,"> Steve said, with obvious sarcasm.

Greg almost growled in frustrated anger. < "Just get out of my head.">

< "We may as well come clean with each other,"> Steve pointed out.

< "You come clean! And while you're at it why don't you tell your teacher your dad beats up on your mom?">

<Just leave it,"> Steve snapped, then countered, < "Why don't you have a good long chat with your father?">

< "He is not my father!"> Greg growled.

< "C'mon Greg.">

< "Look. I don't want to talk about it, alright.">

Stalemate. Neither of them was willing to share any more private information.

Greg took a deep breath. This was not going to work. He tried again. < "Look, Steve. I guess you could say things aren't right at my home right now. Since the breakup that is."> He paused. < "It's been awful. And Germain has been seeing my father behind Mom's back."> Again he stopped.

Steve interrupted. < "You don't have to explain any more. We may not be switched like this for long anyway.">

Greg was silent. He wasn't sure.... < "When is your birthday?"> he asked abruptly.

< "December third.">

< "Same as mine.">

< "How tall are you?">

< "Six two.">

< "Great!">

< "Yeah,"> Greg agreed grimly.

A few more questions only served to further unnerve them. It was scary how identical they were! True they didn't like or dislike the same foods, but they both had almost photographic memories which made schoolwork ridiculously easy. They both loved playing around with computers. Even their weight was the same!

Greg collapsed on the bed thinking furiously. *"This is unreal."*

< "What do you mean?">

With a mutter of disgust, Greg gave up. It was next to impossible to try to concentrate on blocking his thoughts all the time. He let Steve see just how uneasy he was about their mental link. The implication quickly sank in.

Steve voiced their fears. < "What if.... What if we never change back?">

Chapter Five

< "We have to.">

Steve wasn't sure how much conviction Greg actually tried to put in those words—none by the sound of it. He didn't even want to contemplate being black for the rest of his life.

< "Maybe it will happen naturally while we are sleeping."> Greg's mental thoughts were not reassuring. Steve gave a shaky laugh. < "At least we don't have the same personality. That's something different."> He paused. < "Let's not think about it for a while and see what happens.">

Greg was eager to agree. < "What are...?">

< "Your mom left,"> Steve interrupted.

< "Did she go out?">

< "She's in the house but not in the bedroom.">

< "Apartment,"> Greg corrected absently.

< "Huh?">

< "It's an apartment, not a house—a condo really."> Steve sent Greg a blast of irritation.

< "Hey!">

< "Sorry,"> Steve said. He wasn't, not really, and knew Greg picked up his satisfaction when he got Greg's mental promises of revenge.

< "Yeah... yeah.... Sure."> All amusement fled, however, as Greg's mother came back in the room.

< "Greg. Your mom just came in again.">

< "What's she doing? Is she still mad?">

Steve projected a picture of Greg's mother tidying the room and packing away clothes that Germain had thrown down. Thinking that he was asleep, she made no effort to talk to Steve.

< "You can't sleep forever. You need to talk to her. Just get it over with,"> Greg suggested.

< "It's easy for you to say,"> Steve muttered.

Greg winced.

< "Sorry."> Steve tried to mentally clamp down on his fear, knowing how it was affecting Greg. It was hard. He took a couple of deep breaths then blinked and stirred, pretending to wake.

Greg's mother immediately turned to him. "How are you feeling? How is your head?"

"Fine," Steve muttered. "I feel fine." *This is surreal. I can't believe this.*

Greg's mother, Mrs. Martin, took a seat on the bed. "Greg, I know you're still angry that I had them do those tests. But please! You are old enough now. You should at least try to understand." She paused. "I thought I could at least depend on you—first your grades and now this."

She was visibly upset. Steve shifted uncomfortably on the bed. He hated this. And he wasn't sure what she was talking about. "I'm sorry...."

"Sorry!" Mrs. Martin ran a distracted hand through her hair. "Are you in one of those gangs?"

"No!" It was the truth. He wasn't Greg!

"Then why? I don't understand you, Greg."

"Look M...." *What should I call her? I can't say Mrs. Martin.* "I'm sorry. I really didn't think... I guess I was just upset." From what Greg had told him, he recognized that Greg was trying to somehow punish both of his parents by acting out. But just because Greg was a mass of anger and frustration there was no need for him to be mad too. There was no way he was going to take the heat for Greg's dumb acts.

Mrs. Martin was silent for a minute. "Do you understand now why I had to have them do the blood test?"

What blood test? He had no idea what she was talking about. He would ask Greg about the blood testing later. "Yes," he said.

She relaxed. "I got Mr. Brent's message and met with him. He's really sorry Ray got you involved although he thinks this incident may really have shaken Ray up." She paused, then continued. "I hope so. From what he says Ray has had trouble accepting his mother's death. He's been acting up since she died last year." Another pause. "It's not that I mind if you are friends with him, but please don't let him lead you into doing any more stupid acts, okay?"

"Don't worry Mom. Once was enough. I've learned," Steve reassured her.

She took a big relieved breath, then asked curiously. "Did you and Germain have a fight or something?"

"Sort of." He got the impression Greg was just really mad with Germain.

"I wish you boys would learn not to joke over serious matters. I'll leave you to sort things out with Germain. He's worried about you."

That wasn't how Greg saw it, but Steve let that pass. "Sure."

"Do you feel like school tomorrow?"

Actually he didn't. "No."

Mrs. Martin nodded in agreement. "It's Thursday anyway. By Monday you should be okay." She patted his hand before getting up. "Stay in bed. I'll bring you something to eat in a little while."

Steve watched her leave the room. *This was easy.* He relaxed on the bed. All he needed now was his computer. More than likely there was one here but it wasn't in the bedroom and he wasn't yet brave enough to tackle wandering about the house. No way was he leaving this room anytime soon. The book he'd been reading would have to do. Greg had some of his favorite science fictions anyway.

Steve finally relaxed. Greg was going to be furious. But somehow he still felt he had done the right thing. He waited until after dinner before mentally seeking Greg.

Greg immediately responded. < "What happened?">

< "Nothing."> There was no point upsetting Greg until he had to.

< "What do you mean by nothing?">

< "Your Mom and I chatted for a bit then she left. I got dinner in bed.">

< "And nothing happened.">

< "Will you calm down?"> He was getting Greg's panicky disjointed thoughts.

< "What's happened to you so far?">

< "Nothing,">

Greg paused, then, < "Did Germain come in?">

< "He did but he left again.">

< "Where did he go?">

< "I'm not his nanny. I didn't ask him. Did my Mom come in?">

< "No.">

< "Mom should be in anytime now. HE usually comes in late."> Steve was determined to change the subject. He could clearly read Greg's thoughts and Greg was worried. Somehow Greg must have picked up something of his conversation. Some other time he would figure out exactly what. Right now he didn't want to go there, and since Greg seemed reluctant to come right out and say something he definitely wasn't volunteering any info.

Greg finally accepted his change of topic. < "Will they say anything if I stay in bed?">

< "No, I doubt it. I often eat in my room. And if he lets her, Mom will bring you up something to eat.">

< "I'll stay put then."> Greg sounded relieved.

< "Just don't upset my Mom.">

< "What's that supposed to mean?">

< "Don't rag her about leaving him.">

Greg was silent.

< "Did you hear me?">

< "I heard you.">

< "Well?">

< "Well, what?">

Steve got annoyed with Greg's deliberate attempt to evade the issue. < "If you mess things up with my Mom, I'll....">

< "Yeah. You'll what?">

Steve exploded in fury. < "You... you.... You know what I think? I think you want to be white. You want me to be stuck here in this dinky house with your dumb brother while you enjoy my house. I don't think you're even trying....">

An equally furious Greg interrupted him. < "If I was choosing to stay white, I sure as hell wouldn't choose to be in your stupid family. Only an idiot would stay with someone who....">

< "Don't you dare say my Mom's an idiot....">

< "Well she's rich enough to walk out any time she wants to. Since she's still here....">

< "Well your brother is a fool. And your mother is dumb not to know that her own son is seeing his father behind her back.">

Within minutes the argument had sunk to a vicious level of name-calling. Steve knew he should stop. But he was too angry and frustrated to even try. In fact, it was his fury that finally ended the argument. He sent a blast of such pure frustration at Greg that it literally knocked the other boy down. There was absolute silence.

< "Greg!"> *Hell! What have I done?* It was just anger and frustration at fate that had caused him to lash out. He could read Greg's mind pretty clearly and he knew that Greg, while marveling at the novelty of being white, did not want to stay white, at least not in his house. < "Greg? Answer me! Greg?">

< "Go to hell!">

A flood of relief washed over Steve. < "Are you hurt?">

Greg didn't answer but Steve could still feel his

presence and read his thoughts. Greg was still angry, and he also had a massive headache.

< "Sorry."> Steve muttered.

No answer.

< "Greg?">

Abruptly there was again silence from the other end.

Steve hesitated. He knew Greg was angry but not hurt. Maybe he should leave him for a while. After all, Greg was the one who started it by implying that his mother was stupid.

* * * *

The next day Steve waited until the house was empty before getting up. He eased slowly out of the bed. His ribs were still painful and sore. Since he was stuck here, he decided that he might as well find out more about his surroundings. After exploring the room his next stop was the bathroom. Yesterday, he had avoided looking at himself. Today he figured he had to look at himself sometime, so it might as well be now.

For a long while he stood looking at himself in the bathroom mirror. Where did the term 'black' come from anyway, he thought in irritation. His skin was not black – just chocolate brown. Still, he was so dark! And his eyes were black—he looked closer—no, not black, but a very dark brown. But even his palms were darker than his former skin color. Then his hair: it was cropped close to his head in no particular style—just a short cut. He touched the hair on his head hesitantly, finding it surprisingly springy. Yet it was totally different from his real hair. How did he comb it?

The comb slid through easily. For a long time he continued to stare at himself. *This was so weird. I'm black! A minority!* If he showed up at home like this.... Just the thought was mind-boggling. Steve put down the comb and decided he had spent long enough in the bathroom doing nothing. Staring at himself like this was not changing anything. He carefully wrapped his cast arm in plastic, unwrapped the strapping about his chest, and stepped in the shower.

Friday evening was a repeat of Thursday. He had dinner in bed again, but the day came and went without him hearing from Greg. It was now Saturday and Mrs. Martin had washing and cleaning to do. Their washing machine was broken so she left both him and Germain and made an early start to the Laundromat—in the next building.

"When Germain gets awake the two of you can vacuum the rooms," she said. "I should be back in about two hours."

Germain pretended to sleep during the exchange and his mother made no effort to wake him. As soon as she was out of the house Germain got up.

"When Mom comes back tell her I had to go out." He headed for the door.

"What about the vacuuming?" Steve asked.

"If you're so worried about it, you do it."

Steve gave him a disgusted look, which Germain saw but ignored.

After Germain left, Steve hunted for the vacuum, finally finding it in a closet off the kitchen. He couldn't remember actually vacuuming an entire room before, but didn't see how it could be that difficult. As he started, he wondered what Greg would have done. He didn't want any shocked reactions from Greg's mom. Steve hesitated. He had already apologized. No way was he going to contact Greg first. With a shrug he started again. He certainly wasn't going to sit around all day and do nothing.

It wasn't bad, if he didn't bend too much. The apartment had only two bedrooms, a kitchen and eat-in area, a living room and two small bathrooms—one connected to the main bedroom. The worst was having to pick up stuff off the floor every few minutes. The strapping about his chest made bending difficult, and when he forced the issue, he ended up with a stabbing pain in his chest.

There was no television in his and Germain's bedroom but Mrs. Martin had one in her room. There was also a television in the living room. Steve got mad again as he imagined Greg lounging in *his* bedroom watching the TV. Extending his anger to Germain, he deliberately left all of Germain's side of the room un-vacuumed.

When Greg's mother came back, her lack of surprise when he told her Germain had gone out was telling.

"You should insist that he stay and do some work," Steve said.

"I know, I know, but...." Her voice trailed off and she ran a weary hand through her hair. She gave Steve a half smile. "I should have insisted when he was little. I spoiled you both and now I'm beginning to regret it."

Steve took some of the clean laundry from her, turned and moved away. He was beginning to like Greg's mother. But he still did not understand her. She was going to regret not keeping a closer eye on Germain. "Where do I put these?" he asked absently.

She stared at clothes he was holding, "In the drawers."

"Oh." Steve felt like an idiot. Of course Greg would have known where. He moved away. At his home their housekeeper usually packed away the wash.

Throughout the day he could feel Mrs. Martin giving him strange looks every now and again as he made blunders.

When he couldn't figure out how to turn on the stove, she helped, after giving him a peculiar look and murmuring, "I hope that blow to your head isn't causing you to lose your memory. Maybe I should take you back to the doctor."

It was said half-jokingly, but Steve was on the verge of panic. When he burned the eggs and made a mess in the kitchen, she assumed it was because he didn't have the use of his left arm. He knew better. He had never in his life fried eggs. She looked at him strangely when he couldn't find the sugar. She had asked him to mix some juice for lunch. "Greg, maybe you should go back to bed for a while."

"No, M.... Mom. I feel fine. Really." But he could feel his face heating up in embarrassment. He quickly turned to do something that he knew he could do—wash the dishes—but there was no dishwasher in sight. "Where is the dish...?" He stopped abruptly. Maybe he really should stay in bed, he thought as he gave Mrs. Martin a panicky look. Fortunately, she was busy wiping off the counter top and didn't pick up his latest blunder.

"The dish rag is hanging over the drain," she answered.

"Yeah. I see it," Steve said in relief. But he still didn't know where the dishwasher was and he could hardly start opening cupboards to find out. Steve stood looking at the sink full of dirty dishes. He didn't know what to do!

Mrs. Martin turned and saw him just standing, staring at the sink. "Greg. Leave those. I don't want your cast getting wet."

"Okay," Steve agreed. Thank God for the cast. He stood back and watched as she quickly rinsed the dishes and loaded the dishwasher. At least next time he would be able to do them.

Despite the blunders, he survived the day and was even beginning to relax when Germain burst in at about five o'clock. Mrs. Martin was fixing diner and he was enjoying the computer.

"Germain! Where were you all day?" she began.

"I had to meet up with some friends," Germain sounded sullen. "I promised them. I had to go."

"Germain, I'm not going to put up with this...."

"It's not like I'm staying out all night. I'm home, aren't I?"

"Germain, you left this morning at the crack of dawn—without a word of explanation to me or your brother. This isn't a hotel. It's your home. Do you think it's fair that you do nothing...?"

"I do stuff in the house...." Germain's tone was hostile.

Steve let the argument wash over him. It wasn't his business; besides, he didn't want to get involved.

Germain was still angry and sulky during dinner but Steve ignored him and so did Mrs. Martin. The news was on and Steve was not really listening until Germain spoke.

"Whites."

He paused with his fork halfway to his mouth. "What?"

"Some men robbed a jeweler yesterday. As usual, when the crooks are white they don't say the race. If they were black or Hispanic, that's the first thing they would have said."

Steve stared at him blankly—uncomprehending.

Germain seemed unable to pass up the opportunity to taunt. He pressed the issue. "Don't you get it?"

Steve didn't answer. He didn't understand what Germain was getting at but since he didn't want to look dumb he waited for Germain's clarification. He didn't have to wait long.

"They never miss an opportunity to put blacks in a bad light. So the fact that they didn't say it's a black guy that robbed the store means a white guy did it."

"Oh." Steve was nonplussed. Never before had he heard such an analysis of the reasons behind why one's race was mentioned in the news yet another wasn't. He looked at Mrs. Martin, expecting her to disagree, but to his surprise she was nodding.

Convinced that both Mrs. Martin and Germain were paranoid, he refused to join the discussion that followed. Every scrap of news was viewed through the filter of race. Blacks did not have a life! At least Germain was no longer sulking but that did not last long. Toward the end of the meal Germain got mad again when Mrs. Martin grounded him for the next weekend.

"It's only fair, Germain," she said. "Greg did just about all the housework this weekend. Next week it's your turn. You can't expect to live here and do nothing."

"I didn't tell him to do all the vacuuming," Germain began justifying angrily.

"You weren't here," his mother pointed out.

"Well he could have left it.... He...."

"Germain! I really am tired of your excuses."

In a fit of temper, Germain scraped back his chair, jumped up, and slammed into the bedroom.

Mrs. Martin gave Steve a weary look. "I don't know what to do."

Steve hesitated. His mother had never confided her problems—had never asked him for his advice. He couldn't imagine her discussing any adult issue with him. In his household he, the child, did not instruct the adults. He couldn't see his mother and certainly not his stepfather coming to him with a problem. He figured Mrs. Martin must really be depressed to admit she needed help. "Uh.... They have... er... social workers and such... um... maybe they could help."

She sighed. "Maybe.... It did work the last time but I'll have to do something soon. He's getting worse, not better, isn't he?"

"I... I... well," Steve didn't know what to say. Germain *was* out of control. But would Greg have admitted that? Greg hadn't been a saint over the last few months from what he had gathered.

Mrs. Martin patted his arm. "I'm glad, at least, that

you're back to normal." She gave him a quick look. "Greg, I know it has been hard. But try to understand your father."

"Is he...?"

She gave him a puzzled look. "Is he what?"

"My father."

"Oh." She bit her lips. "Yes. I gave him the results of the blood test. Greg, I had to... I'm sorry. There was no other way to give him proof. And I think both of you needed to be reassured that you are father and son despite what he may or may not believe."

"Oh." Steve was trying to absorb this new information. So that was the reason for the blood test.

"I know adjusting has been hard. Are you still mad?"

Steve shook his head. But he would bet anything that Greg would still be mad. *Oh well. There isn't much I can do about that.*

"What did he say?" He was intensely curious but did not really expect an answer.

She turned away. He could see she was still upset.

"You don't have to..." he began.

"No. No. I have to talk about it sometime. I didn't actually speak to him. I just contacted my lawyer and had the papers sent over. I hope he will make it up to you when he gets all the facts."

Steve noted that she did not speak of reconciliation between herself and Greg's father.

"Don't worry, Mom," he reassured, sensing her anguish. "I'm not going to act up again if he doesn't."

She gave him a watery smile, then came over and gave him a quick hug.

Steve helped her wash up, and they shared a comfortable silence. That fact Steve found almost unbelievable. He had never had much contact with blacks. Aleck was the only black kid he came in regular contact with and there were only four other blacks in his grade. Over the years, Aleck and the other blacks in the school had blended neatly into the school's population.

Tentatively, he tried to examine why Aleck's race didn't seem to make any difference. In this family he was intensely conscious of race. Everything seemed to revolve around comparisons of the different races... or discussions of black issues. Although he was not Aleck's best friend, they talked occasionally, and Aleck's talk was no different from the other white kids at school. Maybe when Aleck was in his own home he discussed black issues but Steve sure couldn't remember ever hearing any such discussion at school. In fact, the only times he could remember such issues coming up were during class discussions on civil rights and slavery, plus Barack Obama's presidency.

Steve didn't consider himself racist or anything—it was just how he grew up. He felt comfortable among his own people—people from the same background, people who came from his little part of the world and who were willing to discuss his concerns.

This was why he had felt vaguely uncomfortable during the meal. The conversation and topics were totally unfamiliar. Satisfied with his mental reasoning he relaxed again. But still.... It was so hard to believe; he was in the kitchen helping a black woman wash up the dishes....

* * * *

The next day, Sunday, Mrs. Martin tried to cajole both boys into going to church with her. Germain refused outright. Steve hesitated, then he too declined. More than likely it would be a black congregation. Dealing with a crowd of blacks would be a lot different than handling just two. He didn't think he was up to that just yet. He shied away from the thought of school on Monday. Greg had told him the school was mixed. Still, he was already scared!

As soon as Mrs. Martin left the apartment, Germain slipped out. Steve didn't bother questioning him. He expected Germain to be gone all day and so was surprised when Germain burst into the apartment less than an hour later.

"Greg! Dad wants to see you." Germain said in a rush.

"Dad?" Steve was in the living room watching the television. He looked around, startled. "What do you mean? Dad?"

"It's Dad. He's outside and he wants to see you!"

Chapter Six

"What?" Steve jerked upright.

"Greg, you've got to see him. He's sorry about what he said to you. It was all Mom's fault for letting him think you weren't his son."

"Hell!"

"Can he come in? Will you see him?"

Steve jumped off the sofa. "Damn! Damn!" He didn't know what to do! < "Greg!"> he screamed.

< "What?"> Greg's response was surly. It was clear he was still angry. Steve ignored that. He quickly explained.

< "Hell!">

< "What do I do?">

< "Don't see him."> Greg was definite.

< "But he's outside"> Steve protested.

< "I don't care where he is. I don't want to see him.">

Steve turned to Germain.

Germain was staring at him. "What's up with you?"

It was then that Steve realized that he had simply stood staring in space while talking mentally to Greg. "Forget that. Listen." Steve still hesitated, reluctant to follow Greg's advice. This was wrong.

< "Please Steve. I don't want to see him. *Please!* Tell Germain you can't see him. I'll tell you what. We can try switching back now. C'mon Steve. I wouldn't do that to you.">

Steve sank down on a sofa, the better to think. In truth he hated this.

< "Steve?">

Steve did not reply.

"Greg, what the hell is wrong with you?" Germain was still staring at him.

Steve looked up. Germain was still more puzzled than anything else but if Steve didn't do something soon Germain would begin to think he was crazy. Still, Steve hesitated. *What to do?* He really didn't want to get involved. This was not his problem. Vaguely, he was aware that Greg was reading his chaotic emotions. That, he couldn't help. What he really wanted was to get out of this situation. He didn't want to meet anyone—certainly not a black man who was nothing to him. He gave Germain a desperate look.

"Why did you have to ask him to come here?"

"He wanted to come and I told him you would see him. Greg, can't you just try to understand? You always just take Mom's side. Dad—he's been so upset. He's started drinking; he's so depressed. Why can't you just see him?"

Greg's voice came through. It was calmer than before but still anxious. < "Steve?">

Steve had a throbbing headache.

< "Steve?"> It was Greg again.

< "What?>"Steve said shortly.

< "Let's try and meet after school tomorrow. Maybe

something will happen. Maybe we will be able to switch back when we're closer.">

Steve turned away from Germain's pleading look. "I... I... I can't," he muttered. He felt terrible. *This is not my problem. This is not my problem.* Repeating that phrase did not work. He still felt terrible.

Germain gave him a furious glare. "I wish they'd broken your other arm too," he shouted, before slamming out the door.

Silence.

Steve buried his face in his hands. He was aware of Greg's presence, yet Greg, perhaps sensing Steve's disquiet, did not intrude.

I don't even know the man. This is Greg's problem, not mine. This has nothing to do with the fact that he is black. I don't want Greg getting involved with my family either. Of all the people I had to switch with why did it have to be here? There are tons of white people with problems. Why did I have to get stuck in a black family? He took a deep breath. Greg didn't want to meet with his father anyway, so if Greg were here the same thing would have happened. That logic did not make him feel any better. *I should have gone out.* Greg was bitter and confused. He knew that, and yet he had still followed Greg's advice. *I shouldn't have asked Greg for advice.* For a long time Steve just sat staring blankly at nothing. Finally, he stirred. The deed was done now. There was nothing he could do about it.

< "Where can we meet?"> He knew Greg was still mentally hovering.

They spent a few minutes discussing meeting places. Finally, they decided on a park a mile and a half from Steve's home. The park was about an equal distance from Steve's school so Greg could walk there after school. Steve would have to take two buses then walk to the park.

His was the longer journey but at least the bus stopped near the park. Not that he would object, even if it were a mile away. Not with the possibility that this nightmare could be over. He was finally able to relax. Neither he nor Greg mentioned Greg's father again.

* * * *

Germain got back before Mrs. Martin. After giving Steve a few dirty looks he basically ignored him.

At first, Steve decided to keep out of his way. He stayed in the bedroom while Germain watched television in the living room. There was nothing he could do now and he would be out of here by tomorrow anyway. But after half an hour Steve took some deep breaths; the least he could do was try to help.

For a while he stood at the door of living room, watching Germain. Germain must have been aware of his presence but refused to look away from the screen.

"How is Dad?" Steve finally asked.

No answer.

"If I understood why he needed proof that—"

"What do you care?"

Steve felt his way carefully. Greg had never told him the entire story. He had patched together pieces of Germain's and Mrs. Martin's conversations plus what he got from mentally reading Greg. The quarrel between the Martins he understood but he did not understand why Mr. Martin believed that Greg was not his son.

"He's my dad too," Steve muttered uncomfortably.

Germain finally turned to face him. "So why didn't you see him?"

Steve looked down. "Mom...."

"Mom!" Germain practically screamed in frustration.

"Did he tell you what happened?"

"Yes," Germain glared. "Mom is a.... She was seeing someone else. He showed me pictures of her and some other guy. It was that guy's sister who told him the truth and gave him the pictures. She said Mom and her brother were going to get married. But her brother died. That's why Mom suddenly decided to stay with Dad."

Steve stared. He could not believe.... "But...but... what did Mom say?"

"She never even mentioned this guy to Dad. Never in all these years! So what was Dad to believe?"

Hell! No wonder Germain had no respect for his mother.

"Dad said you were born while he was away," Germain continued. "And you were born early, at least that's what Mom said. Plus, you were a very big baby. At the time Dad never questioned it," Germain finished triumphantly. "So you see? Everything fit. Dad figured Mom was lying to cover up the fact that she got pregnant with this guy she was seeing. But since he was now dead she decided to pass the baby off on Dad."

Steve hesitated. "He shouldn't have told you all this and turned you against Mom." That much he knew. Even if Mr. Martin was right, he should not have given Germain such a one-sided view of the story.

Germain turned away. "He didn't tell me, or show me anything until after I heard him talking with a friend of his."

"Did you ask Mom what really happened?"

"Why should I? She didn't mention the guy to Dad. She *lied* to him."

"Yeah. But I *am* Dad's son so that part at least isn't true."

Germain looked uncertain. "That was just sheer luck," he muttered.

"You should get her side," Steve insisted.

"Not after what she did to Dad."

"Well, what about what he did to her? And to G... me."

"You are just as bad as she is," Germain accused. "Why couldn't you just see him? He came all this way.... He's upset, I tell you."

This was too much. Steve didn't know what to say. Things were really getting complicated. Greg would have to solve this problem. He would have to tell Greg the entire story. Yeah, and watch Greg get mad and blow the whole thing, he thought derisively.

He gave Germain a helpless look. "I don't know," he murmured.

"Can I ask him to come back?" Germain asked eagerly. "Or we could both sneak out and see him tonight."

"NO!"

"C'mon Greg. Dad is really depressed."

"I'll have to tell Mom."

"She'll say no. You know she will," Germain accused. "You're just using her as an excuse not to see him."

That was the truth! Why, oh why did I have to open my mouth and get involved? I'll tell Greg, he'll have to handle this.

"Look. I'll think about it, okay. Maybe tomorrow.... No... not tomorrow.... The next day." Steve relaxed. *Greg should be back by then.*

Germain stared intently at him. "Promise."

"Okay. Okay."

"I'll tell Dad."

* * * *

Later that evening, as Mrs. Martin prepared dinner, Steve followed her around the kitchen. He was trying to work up the courage to ask her about Greg's father. It was the least he could do. Maybe he should tell her that Germain was seeing him. Hopefully she knew already— but how was he to bring up the topic? So intent was he on his thoughts, it was a while before he noticed the odd looks she was giving him.

"Greg, are you sure you're okay?"

"Yeah. I'm fine Mom." He cleared his throat. "Mom?"

"What's the matter?"

I can't do it. I just can't do it. "What's for dinner?"

She gave him a look that clearly questioned his sanity.

Steve felt like a fool. It was obvious to any idiot that she was frying chicken.

"I was just wondering if you wanted me to help with anything."

"Here," She handed him the knife. "Cut up some

salad. Use the tomatoes from the basket," she said, pointing to the basket on the kitchen table, "and make sure to wash the lettuce."

Steve did as he was told. *Why the hell should I worry about any of this? I'll be out of here tomorrow anyway. This is not my problem.*

Chapter Seven

Greg rubbed the side of his face thoughtfully. He did not feel guilty about not letting Steve talk to his father. In fact, he felt a euphoric surge of satisfaction. Revenge was sweet!

Serves him right. You say you don't want to know me—fine. I don't want to know you either. It was a good thing he was in his room when Steve contacted him. He now padded to the bathroom to wash up for bed. Although it was early, he definitely wanted to sleep. Just as he stepped out of the bathroom there was a knock on his bedroom door.

"Steve?"

"Yes."

It was Mrs. Pierce. Since Greg had refused to leave his room all weekend she had brought him food in bed—breakfast, lunch, and dinner. Greg knew she was feeling guilty over the beating he had received. Mr. Pierce, for whatever reason, had not objected. He had visited Greg only one other time, late Saturday, and only to check on Greg's welts. Probably to see if he could make school on Monday, Greg thought uncharitably.

"Can I come in?"

"Yeah."

She came in with a tray. "Pizza. Your favorite."

It *was* his favorite. He grinned reluctantly, and she perched on his bed with the tray. Apart from that first day they had not had much conversation over the weekend. Greg had pretended to be angry, mainly to keep her from lingering in his room to talk. His ploy had worked but he knew he would not be able to keep that up much longer.

He gave her a sideways look. He still felt uncomfortable around her. She smiled. "Well. Aren't you going to eat?"

Greg nodded, hesitated, then sat beside her on the bed, the tray placed between them. He started eating. She watched him.

"Do you want some?"

"You know I don't like pizza," she chided.

He didn't know, but he nodded anyway. He took another quick glance but she was still looking at him so he ducked his head in embarrassment. She was really quite beautiful. Why did she stay with that man? It made no sense.

"Why?" Greg did not realize he had spoken aloud until she replied.

"Steve, please try to understand." She immediately knew what he was talking about.

"I'm trying, but you haven't given me anything to understand yet," Greg said, in genuine frustration.

"Your father and I...."

"Stepfather." Even in a pretend relationship he did not want to be associated with that man.

"Okay."

"Or is he really S... my father?"

For one brief second her face held a look of naked fear and shock—then it was gone. She gave a forced laugh. "Steve. Why on earth would you say that?" Now she looked appalled. "Of course he's your *step*father."

"Good," Greg said. His mind was working furiously. Was that the reason? Was Mr. Pierce Steve's real Dad? But why should she want to hide that fact? Was it something to do with money? Maybe the man who was supposed to be Steve's dad had a lot of money and she would lose it if Steve was not his real son. He took another quick look at her. She looked so sophisticated. He never imagined the very rich could have such problems.

Mrs. Pierce took a deep breath. "I know he has a problem. But he is trying to handle it. Give him a chance."

"Look M... Mom. He has been beating you for over nine years," he suddenly felt angry. How could she allow herself to be abused like that? "Nine years that I know of. Did he start beating you from the time you got married?"

"Steve!"

"Well, did he?"

"What sort of a question is that? Steve, I don't understand you. What's come over you?" In agitation, she stood and wrung her hands.

"I only want answers."

"I've explained to you."

"No. No, you haven't," Greg took a deep breath— it was now or never. "All you have ever done is excuse him and excuse him, or look scared and plead with me. That's not explaining anything."

Mrs. Pierce walked over to the window and hugged herself. "Try to understand," she pleaded.

"I'll try if you give me some answers."

She turned and looked at him almost in bewilderment. "I don't understand you anymore."

"Why do you stay with him?" Greg asked insistently. With his father so often away he had grown up in a virtually fatherless household, which generally placed added responsibilities on the shoulders of the oldest son. Germain had abdicated those responsibilities early on. That had left Greg in charge. It was to him that his mother sometimes turned to for advice. Also, because as an audit accountant she sometimes had to work long hours, it was often left to him to take care of important household matters, even finances.

Growing up, he had loved advising his mother; he discussed problems with her, and had in fact acted as the male head of the household when his father was at sea. As he mentally moved from regarding Steve's mother as a stranger—a rich white stranger—he came to realize that she needed help. Tonight may be his only chance. Maybe he could help her, *and* Steve.

She turned back to the window. "I hoped he would change."

"But now you know he never will. Can we leave him now?"

"Steve... I... I don't know that... I... I've... explained to you.... He's trying...."

Greg interrupted her. His voice now was almost harsh with anger. "You know he'll never change. You know! What hold does he have over you?"

"Stop it! Stop it! I don't know what's come over you, Steve. You've never acted this way before. My God!

You tried to kill him. What did you expect him to do?"

"You know I would never really shoot him," Greg refused to be diverted. "And what about what he has done to you?"

"Steve...." she pleaded.

"Mom, I'm sixteen. I'm not going to stay here and watch him beat you any longer. If he lays another hand on either of us I'm going to call the police."

"Steve! You can't call the police. Please. Listen to me. You can't."

"Why not! Tell me why not and I'll listen," he glared at her. "Is it money? I don't mind if we're poor...."

"God! No! Steve, no, please. I can't talk about it." She turned away from him and buried her face in her hands.

Greg stared at her in frustration. "I'm sorry. I'm sorry." He really hadn't meant to make her cry. For a few minutes he watched helplessly, then he went over and awkwardly placed his arms around her. "I'm sorry." He felt terrible.

"I can't tell you. I'm sorry, Steve." She lifted her head and used her fingers to wipe at her eyes.

Greg released her, walked over to the bed and took a napkin from the tray. He handed it to her silently.

She gave a shaky laugh as she took it. "I'm a pathetic mother, aren't I?"

"Of course not," Greg said automatically. But his eyes were worried as he looked at her. Daniel Pierce definitely had some hold on her, something embarrassing or shameful, and he wanted to find out what. The idea of having a major problem like this hanging over his head and not working at it was alien to him. Maybe after he and Steve changed back he would still be able to help. He definitely intended to try.

"I can't talk about it," Mrs. Pierce said after a long pause. "Just believe me when I say I have to stay with Daniel." Her voice was so low he had to strain to hear it.

"It's okay," Greg came over to pat her shoulder again. "Don't worry. I'll keep quiet."

She nodded. "Maybe one day...."

Greg didn't say anything. He wondered how many times she had said the same thing to Steve.

She seemed to sense his feeling. "You don't know how sorry I am that you got caught up in this. I never imagined...."

Greg interrupted her. He'd had enough excuses for one night. *Time to change the subject.* "Do I have to go to school tomorrow?"

She hesitated, "Daniel wants you to... you know how he is...." She paused again. "A number of your friends called but I told them you had laryngitis."

"Who called?"

She gave a few names. They sounded familiar, so Steve may have mentioned them. Greg sighed and nodded. School was the last thing he wanted to think about right now. He was really dreading it. Being the only black in a... his thoughts skittered to a halt. True, he looked white, but inside he knew he was still the same. He was not sure how to relate with a bunch of rich white kids. It was not just a black-versus-white issue. This was cultural. And *he* was not Steve.

* * * *

The next morning Greg reluctantly contacted Steve. Reluctantly, because he knew that Steve was still upset. But he desperately needed reassurance.

< "Steve.">

< "I don't have much time Greg.">

< "Go over all your friends with me again.">

< "Are you a retard? It's past six.">

Greg was silent.

< "Okay, look in my Yearbook.">

< "Where is it?"> Greg asked, smiling at the note of long-suffering in Steve's voice.

Steve directed him to the desk and bookshelf.

< "Okay,"> Greg said, after a brief check. < "I found it."> He rummaged around in the desk. < "Steve. Do you have your birth certificate?">

< "Birth certificate? You don't need my birth certificate.">

< "I was just wondering."> Greg hesitated. He kept a tight rein on his thoughts, not wanting to tell Steve his theory. < "Have you ever seen it?">

< "Of course I've seen it. What are you getting at?">

< "I'm just curious, that's all."> He hastily improvised. < "I wanted to check the times of our birth and so on.">

< "Oh."> Steve did not sound overly interested. < "Well I don't know. I would have to ask Mom. It's probably in the safe in *his* office. Look Greg, I gotta go. Don't contact me during the day unless it's an emergency. It's too distracting. Germain already thinks I'm going crazy.">

< "Why? What happened?">

< "When he brought home your dad, I was talking to you and staring blankly at nothing—with him standing right in front of me. Look. I'm late. I'll talk to you later.">

* * * *

Thinking of ways to get at the safe kept Greg from worrying about his first day at Steve's school. Mrs. Pierce dropped him off and he slowly walked toward the buildings. School was a sprawling collection of buildings set on manicured lawns. Greg stared as he approached.

"Steve!" A lanky guy was approaching. "I called you on Friday but your mom said you'd lost your voice. What happened?"

"Some bug, I guess," Greg muttered, as he quickly ran through all the information Steve had provided about this friend. His name was John Erickson but he was called Jack. They were good friends but not best buddies. Like Greg, Steve had no true friend. Jack followed him into the school.

"Well, you missed out."

"Missed out on what?"

"The party—at Paula's house."

"Oh," Steve hadn't told him about any party. "So what happened?"

He didn't have to worry. Jack had no problem filling him in with all the latest gossip. Paula was a classmate and on Saturday she'd held a lavish party—inviting everyone from their AP and honors classes. They were in the first period before Greg got Jack to stop. Somehow, Greg had a feeling Steve did not generally tolerate Jack's nonstop chatter, but since he wanted to speak as little as possible he was more than eager to put up with it.

After the nervous tension he had worked up, school was a complete letdown. He didn't talk much, but everyone assumed that was because his throat was still sore. On first impression Greg thought the kids were uniformly friendly even to the one black in the class—the guy Aleck. It was during lunch that he realized there were definite cliques.

Steve generally sat with three other guys. Greg would have felt more comfortable sitting with Aleck's group but realized he could not make so blatant a change. Besides, Aleck's group wouldn't necessarily accept him.

Steve's group of four was considered the brains of their grade. They were all high honor students—a reputation that Greg gathered Steve was very proud of. One guy in the group—Tony—flaunted both his brains and his wealth, and amused himself by making what he no doubt considered humorous jokes. Greg didn't see the jokes as funny. As far as he was concerned, Tony was a bully and his jokes were derogatory or racist.

How does Steve put up with him? He bit his lips to prevent a rude retort. *Control yourself. This is just for today. I can do it for one day.* But there was worse to come. Tony seemed to reserve his taunts for Aleck—the black guy—and another guy, Chris, who had a stutter. Greg was sure Tony wasn't really racist but he seemed to like picking on those unable to defend themselves from his taunts.

He got up abruptly after Tony made another derogatory comment, this time about Aleck's hair. The other two guys were laughing and looked up at him in surprise. Greg muttered something and walked off. *Let*

Steve deal with this.

As he turned a corner of the hallway, he spotted Aleck. Greg was tempted to stop and talk but changed his mind. Striking up a friendship made no sense since Steve would be unlikely to continue it.

"Hi," he said as they passed.

Aleck gave a friendly nod but did not stop.

Jack came running up to him. "What's up with you?"

"Nothing."

"Nothing? You just walked off"—Jack was giving him an incredulous look—"and snubbed Tony like that."

"Too bad for Tony."

"What!"

"I don't like his jokes. Okay?"

"Don't like...." Jack stared. "You never said that before."

"Well I'm saying it now."

Jack was silent for a minute. "I know what you mean. But... you know Tony. He doesn't mean any harm."

"Well good for him, but I don't have to listen to them."

"I told him you didn't mean anything. But he's mad, you know."

"Good!"

"He may not invite you to his place."

"Fine by me," Greg said. But he felt a twinge of guilt. If it was something important, Steve was going to have to do some groveling.

Jack gave him a baffled look. "I don't believe you. Everyone wants to get invited to Tony's place. Just last week we were planning that computer challenge game since he has four computers in his room."

"Look, Jack. Change the subject, will you?" Greg was tired of discussing Tony. Steve could correct any misunderstanding tomorrow. "Maybe tomorrow I'll feel like talking to Tony."

Jack let it slide but Greg could see he was not happy. He, Tony, Jack and the other guy, Bill, all had classes together so there was no way for Greg to avoid Tony. And Tony definitely was not happy with him. Towards the end of the school day Tony began making snide comments about him, first to the other two guys, then to the class in general.

Oh, no! What have I started?

He couldn't wait for school to let out. At the final bell he avoided Jack and started the walk to the park. Although it wasn't far, he had decided that he would prefer waiting there versus staying at school for the game and sitting with Jack or any of the others.

* * * *

Later that afternoon, Greg sat on a bench in the park and waited for Steve. *Five! How much longer should I wait?* He'd told Mrs. Pierce that he would stay to watch track practice at school and take the late bus home. There had also been a baseball game at the park so for over an hour he'd at least been entertained. Now, with the game over, the park was getting deserted. There were a few random bikers and hikers and the tennis court was still occupied but he was the only one in the immediate area.

Just as he was about to give up, he saw Steve

approaching. Greg stared. He was looking at himself! Steve wore a similarly engrossed look.

"Nothing is happening," Steve's voice was filled with despair.

They were close now, less than a yard apart. "Maybe we should touch, or something," Greg suggested.

He tentatively started to reach for Steve's shoulder but stopped as he felt something....

Steve's eyes widened. He must have felt it too.

"What's happening?"

Greg frowned. "I don't know." He paused. "Hey! I can read your mind." Greg did not hide his delight.

Steve abruptly backed away.

Greg continued grinning as he felt Steve's effort to close off his thoughts. "We're equal now," he said.

"Equal!" Steve screamed. "You think this is a joke. I hate this. I hate this." Suddenly he backed away completely, turned and ran towards one of the trees. He began slamming his closed fist on the trunk. "Damn! Damn! Damn! I don't want to stay black."

His thoughts were wide open and Greg could feel his desperation. He staggered as he also began feeling Steve's pain.

He cradled his hand in agony. "Shit! Steve! Stop!"

Steve stopped abruptly, dropped his backpack and sank down to the ground, his head buried in his hands.

Free of Steve's pain, Greg sat down and examined his hand. Surprisingly, it was not bruised. But it was still painful to the touch. He stared at Steve. Meeting like this had linked them more, not less! Since Steve was still consumed with despair, Greg stretched out on his back on the bench and stared at the sky. What the hell were they going to do? Maybe they should take their chance with telling someone?

< "NO!">

Greg jerked up at the mental command. It was Steve. And his eyes were suspiciously red. "Why not?"

"Do you want to end up in some psycho ward?" Steve stood and kicked violently at a stone.

"I could prove I am Greg by telling about my life. My mother...."

"We met here. They would just say that we exchanged information about each other. Besides there's the telephone. We could have spent months planning this. And who do think would ever believe us?"

"I still think...."

"No! No! NO!"

"You don't want anyone to know you're black," Greg concluded. Steve's thoughts were angry, jumbled, and confused. Although he was trying, untangling them was next to impossible.

"Get out of my head!" Steve turned on him in fury, "I don't want you reading my mind."

"Fine," Greg agreed calmly. "I'm not going to read you mentally if you don't read me."

Steve took a deep breath. "I still think that if we tell anyone they will think we're crazy."

"Maybe," Greg was noncommittal. "Telling might be our only option. We can't continue like this."

"If you tell...," Steve began threateningly, but paused at the challenging look Greg was giving him.

"Yes...?"

"It's easy for you...."

"How is it easy for me? You tell me how." Greg was so angry about Steve's attitude that he stood up. "I get to go to a school where I don't know anyone. And don't know what to say to them. I get to live in a family where I am likely to get whipped if I don't stay out of the way. Tell me how it's easy for me."

"You are not black."

"Yeah?" Greg could only stare at Steve in astonishment. "Well I was black for sixteen years. I know exactly what it's like being black."

Steve turned away. "I had to walk miles to get here," he said with extreme exaggeration. "And for nothing."

"You know what your problem is, Steve?" Greg was still seriously annoyed. "Deep down you know that whites have a big advantage in this country. But you just can't admit it. Now you are living as a black and the facts are smacking you in the face. If blacks and whites were so equal you would have no problem being black."

"That's not how I feel." Steve growled. "I like your mother."

"Whatever...."

"It's not just black and white. I wouldn't want to live in a white family where I didn't even know the people either. This has nothing to do with race."

"It has everything to do with race!"

"Okay!" Steve said aggressively. "Okay! Let's talk about race. Do you know how boring it is to listen to your brother moan day in day out about how everyone discriminated against him? If he went to pee and missed the toilet he would probably blame it on race."

"Can you blame him? Do you know what it feels like to not have to consider race? On my way here I went into a store and no one followed me around. No one acted as if I was a criminal about to make off with half the store. It felt weird and I liked it! Do you know what it would do to the self-esteem of blacks it they didn't have to worry about being put down because of their color? You whites take everything for granted. You sit down with your little group and criticize anyone who isn't like you. Take your friend Tony. He's a bully and he picks on anyone who is different...."

"That's not true," Steve interrupted. "You don't know what Aleck did to him once. Aleck deliberately splashed him with fruit punch at a party. That's why Tony hates Aleck. Not because of his race. And saying, 'you whites,' is a racist statement as far as I'm concerned. You just keep assuming things about me—about whites. You don't know anything. You are just trying to put words in my mouth," Steve was now yelling. "You don't know how I feel. I just want to get back to my family." Steve sank down to the ground and pulled up his knees, wrapping his arms around them, cast and all. He stared blankly at the park benches and repeated in a quieter voice, "All I want is to get back to my family."

He had been scared of going out to school that morning. As far as he was concerned he would be alone and friendless. He seriously considered hanging out at a library somewhere. The only reason he didn't was because of Mrs. Martin. He did not want to upset her again. Besides Ray's father arranged to drop him off at school every morning until he got out of the cast. Ray's aunt would pick him and

Ray up from school in the evenings. Nothing Steve had said could dissuade Mr. Brent from this course of action because he still felt that Ray was mostly responsible for Greg's injury.

To be safe, Steve tried being as unobtrusive as possible. In classes he virtually clung to Ray. He knew that his behavior was surprising Ray, and at first he was afraid Ray would vanish on him. But Ray didn't; in fact, Ray seemed delighted. And since Greg and Ray were not friends, Steve had no problem striking up a friendship. Steve was even shocked to find himself liking Ray, even though it was like pulling teeth to get Ray to talk about himself. On the way home they had even arranged to stop off at Ray's home the next day. But that was just one day! Steve couldn't imagine continuing day after day. He just couldn't!

What am I going to do?

Chapter Eight

This can't be happening to me, Steve thought in despair. *Why can't I wake up and find that this is only a dream?*

Greg was again sitting on the bench, silently staring at nothing and Steve didn't know what else to say. The whole situation was too depressing. The only thing that had gotten him through the day was the thought of changing back this evening. Now that hope was gone.

It had been a long silence. Greg suddenly spoke up. "Steve. I've been thinking."

Steve didn't answer. He was just too discouraged.

Greg leaned back on the bench and continued. "We only started getting each other's thoughts a week ago. Before that I had a sort of...." He paused. "I could tell how my dad was feeling—always. That disappeared when I started linking with you. Were you linked with anyone?"

Steve stirred. "My mother." He had been sort of linked with his mother all his life. He could always tell whenever *he* started beating her—even at night. That was why he was looking for the gun that night. He had been unable to sense his mother and he got scared. His worst thought was that his stepfather had killed her. That was why he'd crept out of his room. When he realized his stepfather was beating her again, he'd sort of snapped.

"Do you still have the link with your mom?"

Steve shook his head. He didn't know what Greg was getting at and was feeling too depressed to care.

"Steve, will you snap out of it. Think about this for a minute. We were both linked with someone who..." he paused, then continued quietly, "You care about your mother and I cared about my dad until...." he stopped. "I think we both needed help," he paused again. "Somehow we needed help and accidentally called each other."

"So how does that help us now?"

"I don't know...." In silence, Greg stared at the tree. Finally he continued. "I... my dad.... Living with all of that was driving me crazy. I... I know I wanted to get out. Perhaps we both just needed a break from our problems," Greg suggested.

Steve rubbed his face tiredly. "Greg, this still doesn't help us."

Greg sat up. Almost hesitantly he asked, "What would you do in my case?"

"Talk to your father," Steve said promptly.

"No!"

"Look, Greg. Regardless of what he did, he's still your father. Give him a chance to tell his side of the story. Did you ever find out why he thought you weren't his son?"

"No," Greg's voice was low. Steve had to strain to hear him.

"Well, I know I would at least want to know what happened." He didn't want to tell Greg. Not yet. Greg really needed to want to know, and he didn't think Greg was ready to deal with the facts.

"No," Greg disagreed. "You don't know what you're talking about. You weren't there when it all happened. You didn't hear what he said to me. I don't ever want to talk to him again."

"There are programs...."

"No! And if you talk to him...."

"There is nothing you could do to stop me," Steve finished.

Greg stood up and turned away. He grabbed his backpack from the bench then started walking towards the park exit.

Steve watched him. *Hell!* He really didn't mean to hurt Greg's feelings. It was just that... this was so frustrating! "Greg!" he called.

No answer. Greg just kept on walking.

Steve raised his voice. "Greg. Come back. I didn't mean it like that."

Greg only paused before continuing. "It's getting late. I have to get back." He did not look around.

Steve jumped to his feet and hurried after him. "Okay. Okay. I promise I'm not going to rush and do anything. Okay?"

Greg sighed. "I know it's not your problem."

"You're wrong. It *is* my problem." Steve took a breath. Getting mad and feeling sorry for himself wasn't helping any. "At least now it is. What else were you going to say?"

Greg looked up at the sky. "It's getting dark. I'll walk you to the bus stop."

"You weren't finished. You were going to say something else, weren't you?"

"You're not going to like it."

"Probably not, but I promise not to punch you out."

"Let's walk." Greg forced a smile.

Steve returned to where he had dropped his backpack, picked it up, then rejoined Greg. They walked in silence a while, then Greg said, "I think Mr. Pierce may be your father and your mother is hiding it."

"NO! No way!"

"Steve. Think about it."

"No. That's why you asked about my birth certificate, isn't it? Well, you needn't worry. I know what's on my birth certificate. It says my father is Harold Chadwell."

"It could be forged."

"NO!"

"Will you just think about it for a second? He could have helped your mother fool this guy, Harold Chadwell. It could have been for the money—inheritance—whatever."

"No! NO! You're saying my mother has been lying all these years.... NO!" Steve was furious. He stopped and grabbed at Greg's arm, but Greg jerked away thinking Steve was about to hit him. Because of his action Steve was only able to hold on to his sleeve. Nevertheless, the action halted Greg. "My mother would never do such a thing. Never! And I would rather die than have that man as a father."

"Alright. Alright. Calm down."

"Well you'd better think up some other theory." Steve released Greg's sleeve and they resumed walking.

"But she *is* scared of something," Greg insisted.

"I know that. But what you suggested...."

"Okay, I'll think of something else." He paused.

"You said the safe was in his office, right?"

"Yeah. And you'd better not be thinking of going in there. He'll murder you."

"I'll be careful. Where in the office?"

Steve gave him a mental picture, complete with the sound of a waterfall his stepfather had in the office.

Greg nodded. Then said, "Do you realize what you just did?"

"What?" Steve wasn't in the mood for riddles.

"You were able to send me a picture image with sound. I think when we got close we increased our mental link."

"Oh, no!" Steve tried again to send a sound mentally. Greg was right. He could. "Just don't come too close to me again," he warned Greg. "God knows what will happen if we actually touch each other."

Greg grinned. "So what is your stepdad's usual routine?" he asked, going back to his original question.

"He gets up at six, leaves at seven to get the seven-thirty train. Then he gets in at six-thirty or seven. Sometimes he has business and gets in later and sometimes he has to go out of town. If he is leaving town that would be your best time to search the office but usually he locks it."

"Don't you find that odd, that he would lock his office? I think that means he has something to hide."

Steve thought for a minute. "He has always locked it when he's not there. I never thought about it. He's warned me not to go in there because he has lots of papers that he doesn't want disturbed."

"What about cleaning?"

"When Laura cleans, he's always there or close by, watching her."

"He's hiding something," Greg concluded.

"Just be careful," Steve warned. "We don't want to get hurt. Who knows what will happen if one of us got hurt."

"The other would feel it," Greg's tone was dry.

"What do you mean?" Steve stared.

"When you were banging your hand against that tree, I felt it."

"Mentally?"

"That too. But I felt the pain in my hand. It's ok now but at the time thought my knuckles were crushed."

Steve looked as Greg's flexed and opened his hands. "Sorry."

Greg nodded. They were at the bus stop. "That's another thing that changed when we got close."

Steve just gave him a glum look.

"Did you check the bus schedule?" Greg obviously decided not to pursue the topic further.

"Yeah." Steve fished into his backpack. "One should be here in ten minutes."

"I'll wait," Greg decided. He flashed Steve a mocking grin. "Since you're black you stick out like a sore thumb in these parts."

"Very funny," Steve said. But he couldn't help a return grin. Then he became thoughtful. *I've changed! A while back, such a joke would have had me fuming.*

"You're not as angry," Greg agreed.

"Damn it Greg, you were reading my thoughts again."

"No," Greg protested. "You were giving me your thoughts."

"Yeah? And there's a difference?"

"Remember when you used to get my thoughts if I didn't block them."

"Hell!" Steve said. Sure he remembered. "Another change," he said grimly. "And I don't know whether this is a good or bad sign," he muttered.

"Nothing could get worse."

"Don't say that," Steve warned.

Greg laughed. "Alright, I'll take it back. Oh, before I forget again. Who exactly is Tony?"

"What do you mean?"

Greg gave him a considering look. "You know what I mean, Steve. How he acts—I'd say everyone in that school must have rich parents, yet he acts like he is the only rich kid in the school."

"His parents are probable the richest. His mother inherited millions from her parents. And his father is the owner of Manelli—the perfume company. His grandfather founded the company."

"Shit! Manelli perfumes!"

"Yeah."

"I dissed him at lunch."

"Why did you do that?" Steve gave Greg an irritated look

"I wasn't going to take it while he dished out insults."

"He insulted you? But... we're friends...."

"He insulted blacks."

"He insults everybody. C'mon Greg. He doesn't

mean anything by his jokes."

"I didn't like them."

"That's a dumb attitude to take since he's not even going to understand, considering that right now you're white."

"Too bad. When we switch back, you can make it up with him."

"I don't believe this." Steve threw up his right arm in disgust. He started to say more but could see from Greg's facial expression that arguing would be useless. "You're going to regret your attitude. Tony can be mean. And he runs to his mommy whenever he wants to get anything."

"Your bus is coming," Greg interrupted.

"You'll see," Steve warned as he hopped on the bus.

"Bye," Greg called, grinning.

Chapter Nine

Greg watched the bus for a while then, after hitching his backpack a little higher, he turned and started back to Steve's house. Because he made no effort to hurry, the walk took about an hour. It was after seven when he finally got home.

"Steve! My God! Where were you?" Mrs. Pierce met him at the door.

"Is that him?" he heard Mr. Pierce's voice.

"Yes. Yes." Steve's mother turned to him again. "Are you hurt? What happened?"

"Nothing happened."

"But where were you?"

"I went to the park. I watched a game. I stopped to chat with someone I met there then I walked home." Greg dropped his bag by the door. He couldn't understand what the big deal was.

"None of your friends knew where you were," she accused, as he came further into the house.

"I told you I was going to watch a game."

Mr. Pierce approached. "I don't know what's got into you, Steve, but I'll not have you scaring your mother like this again. Why didn't you answer your cell?"

"I turned it off. I didn't want it ringing during the game." Actually he'd turned it off so he wouldn't even be tempted to answer any calls.

"Do something dumb like this again and you'll be grounded for a month. Is that clear?"

"Yeah. I heard you," Greg said dryly. As he moved to pass the older man, he felt like asking, 'And what do you do to her when you hit her?'

"Don't take that attitude with me," Mr. Pierce warned as he moved closer to Greg.

Greg was silent. Mrs. Pierce hovered in the background. Greg looked at her face. There was a new bruise just below her right eye.

"Did he hit you again?" he burst out angrily, and without thinking.

Whoosh! Greg ducked just in time to avoid Mr. Pierce's fist. Mrs. Pierce screamed. "Oh God! Daniel! For God's sake!" She tried to reach Greg but Mr. Pierce grabbed her arm.

Greg backed away, warily. His eyes darted between Mr. Pierce and Steve's mother. *Should I escape now? Should I wait?*

"No!" Holding firmly to his wife with one hand, Mr. Pierce pointed a warning finger at Greg. "I'm warning you; watch your mouth."

"Or what? What will you do? Whip me again or use me as a punching bag like you use her?" Greg didn't know what had come over him. He just couldn't stop himself; he was so angry that she'd been hit once again.

Mr. Pierce doubled his fist again.

"You hit me, and I swear I'll hit you back," Greg

warned as he backed further away. His heart was pounding.

< "Greg? What the hell is wrong?">

Greg hesitated but then reluctantly opened his mind so Steve could see the scene.

< "Damn it Greg! What happened?">

Greg couldn't answer. Mr. Pierce had started towards him. He turned around in panic then yanked a large elephant figurine off the entrance table. He held it threateningly. The older man stopped and started cursing violently. Suddenly turning, he backhanded Mrs. Pierce across the mouth.

She screamed as she stumbled and fell. "Daniel!"

"See what he's become. See!" The man shouted. "God damn you both." He turned his fury on Greg. "Put that down and get over here now or I swear I'll kick her."

Greg's gaze darted frantically between them. Mrs. Pierce was lying on the ground supporting her body with her arm. Her eyes were dilated in fear. *He'll kill me.* If looks could kill, he knew he would already be dead. There was no way he would survive if Mr. Pierce actually got his hands on him.

< "Greg do it! Do it! Do as he says. Oh Shit! Do it! He'll kill her! Greg!"> Steve was screaming mentally at him.

Greg slowly started lowering the arm holding the elephant. He meant to put it down—truly he did, but something inside snapped. He lifted his arm and threw it.

The heavy ceramic slammed into Mr. Pierce's jaw. The man staggered, lost his balance and fell. Greg did not wait. He ran over to Mrs. Pierce, grabbed her arm and pulled her with him up the stairs.

"Steve! No! Wait!" She tried to protest.

"Come on!" Greg urged as he pulled her. They ran down the upstairs corridor and into his bedroom. After slamming and locking the door, he turned to Mrs. Pierce. She was sitting on his bed, her hands covering her face, quietly weeping.

Steve was still screaming in his head. < "That was so dumb, Greg. How could you do that? Oh Shit!">

< "Just shut up! Shut up!"> Greg finally stormed back.

Steve calmed down, slightly. < "What happens now?">

< "Hopefully by tomorrow he'll have calmed down and will realize he can't kill us both."> Greg went over to the bed, sat, and placed a comforting arm around Mrs. Pierce. "He will calm down by tomorrow," he repeated reassuringly, as he patted her shoulder.

"Oh Steve. I'm sorry. I'm sorry." She turned her face onto his shoulder.

Greg's heart rate was slowly returning to normal.

< "He wouldn't have killed you,"> Steve said.

< "Yeah sure,"> Greg snorted. < "I wouldn't want to bet my life on that. You didn't see his face?">

Steve said nothing.

They waited for what seemed like hours, but when Greg checked the clock, only fifteen minutes had passed. No one knocked on the door. In fact, the house remained eerily silent.

< "Where is Laura?">

< "She usually goes to her apartment in the evening.">

< "Where is that?">

< "Didn't you go outside?"> Steve sounded irritated. < "It's over the garage. It's a one bedroom apartment.">

Greg ignored the sarcasm. < "Where are you?">

< "Still on the second bus. I should be coming to my stop soon.">

< "Be careful when you get out. Walk in the middle of the street. It's late.">

< "I'm black, remember?"> Steve was definitely irritated.

Greg couldn't work up a smile. He was too worried. < "What do I do now?">

< "You got yourself into this mess—get yourself out! And you had better not get my mother hurt.">

< "Fine! Be that way.">

< "Damn it Greg. How could you hit him?">

< "Because I saw his face. Maybe he didn't really mean to kill. But the way he was mad he could easily have killed me accidentally.">

< "Alright. Alright. It's done now.">

Steve's mother lifted her head. Greg scanned her face carefully. "He hit you this evening, didn't he?"

She sighed wearily, "Yes. He.... He was upset when I tried to defend you."

"Defend me for what?"

"Being late."

"Oh." He stared at her in distress.

"Don't worry about it," she patted his arm. "It's not your fault. I don't think he really means to hurt me. He's just... he just can't control his temper. He's like a little boy hitting out when he can't get his own way."

Greg said nothing. As far as he was concerned, little

boys got punished when they hit out. Big boys should be punished too.

Steve came back, clearly upset. < "She has never ever confided in me like this.">

Greg ignored Steve. "Is there a friend you could call to come over?"

"What do you mean?"

He got up, went over to the phone and lifted the receiver. There was no dial tone. "Never mind," he said.

"What?"

"He must have taken the phone off the hook. There is no dial tone and my cell phone is in my bag downstairs."

"He's afraid you'll call the police." She was shaking her head in despair. "And my cell phone is in the bedroom."

"Maybe there's another way." He went over to the window and looked out.

"What are you thinking?"

"I'm going to climb out."

"What?" Mrs. Pierce exclaimed. "Steve, no! You could get hurt."

< "I hope you know what you're doing,"> Steve muttered.

Greg answered Mrs. Pierce, "I should be okay."

Just as he started pulling the sheet off the bed there was a loud rapping on the door.

"Steve? Melissa?"

Greg stopped. Mrs. Pierce looked up in dismay. "Oh God! Oh God!"

"Listen to me, Steve. I've disconnected the phones so you can't call out. Now come out of the bedroom and be reasonable. I'm sorry I lost my temper. Melissa? Melissa!

Talk to him. I'm not going to hurt either of you."

"I think he means it," Mrs. Pierce said shakily. "Steve, please. If we come out now, things may calm down but it could get worse if we don't. *Please.*"

"Melissa?"

Greg hesitated. < "Steve? You know him better. What do you think?">

< "I don't know. I don't know."> Steve's voice was a mental whisper.

"We're coming out," Mrs. Pierce said, after giving Greg a pleading look. She walked over to the door and unlocked it.

Greg stood back. He really didn't know what to expect. His heart was pounding again. They had no means of protecting themselves. Nothing.

Melissa Pierce slowly opened the door.

He was just standing there. He stared broodingly at them. No, not at his wife—at Greg.

Greg stared back. Mr. Pierce turned to his wife. "Will he call the police?"

"No. No. He won't," she said, after giving Greg a quick look.

Greg said nothing.

Mr. Pierce nodded once, then reached for his wife's arm. "Come to bed."

"If she has any more bruises on her tomorrow I *will* call the police," Greg said—that threat, he realized, was Mr. Pierce's greatest fear. He could control his wife through whatever hold he had on her, but now he could not control her son—him!

Daniel paused, but he did not stop, nor did he

answer.

Greg watched them walk to their bedroom then went over and kicked the door shut.

< "You are a moron. You know that, don't you?"> Steve muttered.

< "What do you think? Will he hit her again?"> Greg asked, ignoring Steve's mutter.

< "Not tonight. I don't think.... You are probably right. He's afraid of what you might do.">

< "I hope so,"> Greg exhaled. His joints felt stiff with tension. < "I'm going to take a hot bath and head for bed.">

< "Okay. Just don't do anything else for the night. I almost had a heart attack just now.">

< "How did you know something was up?">

< "Your fear almost paralyzed me,"> Steve baldly stated. < "One minute I was relaxing and enjoying the view—the next thing I knew I was swamped with fear."> He paused. < "This is my stop.">

< "Okay. Look, bye for now. I'm heading for a bath.">

< "Let me know...."> Steve began.

Greg understood. < "Sure.">

* * * *

The next morning Mr. Pierce was sitting at the breakfast table when Greg got there.

"Morning, Steve," he lowered his paper and silently watched as Greg took a seat two chairs away.

Putting the paper aside, he lifted his coffee cup and took a sip. "Your mother should be down shortly," he said.

Greg nodded.

Laura, their housekeeper, came up to him. "Morning Steve. What are you having?"

"Good morning Laura. I... I...." Greg was uncomfortable. He felt as if he was in a restaurant or something. Steve had explained the routine to him and he had gone through the same thing yesterday but he was still uneasy. "Just waffles and juice."

"Where exactly did you go yesterday?" Mr. Pierce asked as Laura left them. He seemed to be making a genuine effort to be pleasant.

Greg decided to play it safe and give non-risky answers. "I went to the park and watched a baseball game. I was chatting with someone I met there and didn't notice the time."

"Why didn't you call home when you saw it was getting late?"

In truth Greg hadn't thought of calling. "Sorry."

"What park?"

"Lincoln Park."

"Who were you talking to?"

"I didn't ask the guy his name."

"Someone from your school?"

"No."

"Do you really expect me to believe all this bullshit?"

Greg didn't answer. Laura was coming with his waffles and juice. He thanked her with a smile and started eating.

"Well?" Mr. Pierce demanded. He was definitely losing his earlier cool.

"It's the truth."

Mr. Pierce scowled. "You've been acting different lately. I don't know what's got into you but it had better not be drugs."

Greg continued eating. He did not respond.

"I'm going to authorize the school to search your locker for drugs."

Although angry at the implications Greg refused to let it show. He shrugged. "Fine by me."

Mr. Pierce gave him a steely-eyed look. "And another thing: I heard you snubbed Tony. Did you?"

Greg was saved from an immediate response by the entrance of Mrs. Pierce.

He stared at her face but could see no new bruises. In fact, he didn't even see the old ones. Her make-up was perfect.

She gave him a nervous smile, then her gaze immediately darted back to Mr. Pierce.

"Good morning."

"Morning, Mom," Greg's smile was encouraging.

Mr. Pierce grunted, then continued his questioning. "I want to know why he snubbed the Manelli kid."

To Greg's surprise Mrs. Pierce sided with her husband. "Oh Steve, how could you? Tony's mother was on the phone with me and she was very upset."

Greg could not believe they were making a big thing of this. "I didn't like his jokes," he admitted.

"I don't believe this. You don't like his jokes so you are going to ruin a good relationship?" Mr. Pierce sounded incredulous.

"Just humor him, dear," Mrs. Pierce advised, as she drank her coffee. She waved Laura away. "No thanks,

Laura. I'm really not hungry this morning. Coffee is fine."
Then to Greg: "You know how his mother is. And I need
her contribution for the fundraiser for cancer research next
month."

Greg stared at them. No power on earth was going
to get him to be best buddies with Tony Manelli. He stuffed
the last of his waffle in his mouth. "It's getting late, Mom.
Can we go now?"

"Did you hear your mother?" Mr. Pierce demanded.

"Yeah, I heard." Greg pushed back his chair and
stood.

Mr. Pierce gave him another hard stare before
turning to his wife. "I don't know what's gotten into him,
but I don't like it. You'd better have a talk with him. I can't
afford to lose the Manelli account."

She gave him a swift, nervous nod then shocked
Greg by going over and giving her husband a quick kiss.

Greg turned away and headed out to the garage.
How could she stand him?

While waiting for her to come out, he quickly
checked in with Steve. Steve was in a hurry and only wanted
to know how his mother was. Once Greg had reassured
him he backed out. Greg got into the car to wait.

Mrs. Pierce pressed the automatic garage door
opener as she slipped behind the wheel of her BMW. The
car eased out into the driveway. She did not start speaking
until they were on the road.

"Steve, I don't understand you. You've changed."

Greg tensed.

She glanced at him when he did not respond. "I'm
sure it wouldn't hurt to be polite to Tony."

Greg rested his elbow on the window's edge and propped up his chin. "Will he beat you if I'm not?"

"Steve! What sort of question is that?"

"Well? Will he?" Greg insisted.

She pursed her lips. "You *have* changed. You were never so... so... audacious before."

"Are you going to answer?" he asked calmly.

"I'm your mother," she said indignantly. "You shouldn't speak to me like that."

Greg turned and stared out the window. *You're not my mother, but I sort of like you and I would like you a lot better if you stood up to that man.* Without turning to her he continued to press the issue, "That means he would."

"Steve. Please."

Greg moaned silently as he realized that she was going back to her old pleading technique. That was not going to stop him. This time he wanted answers. "Is he my real father? Is he blackmailing you?"

"Steve!" Mrs. Pierce slammed on the brakes as the car swerved violently. "Oh my God!" She shakily pulled the car over to the curb. Once they stopped her hands dropped to her lap. She then leaned back, her head resting on the headrest. "Oh God. Oh God. Steve, I'm so sorry."

"Could you please just tell me the truth?" He stared earnestly at her. "Please."

For a long moment he thought she wouldn't answer. Then she began haltingly, "Steve. This isn't the time. You have school."

"What you have to say can't be any worse that what I've been thinking. Please tell me. I don't care even if I miss first period. I need to know." He hesitated, then touched her arm reassuringly. "Please, Mom."

Again she was silent. Greg looked at her quietly then turned away to stare out the window. *Please tell me,* he pleaded silently. *Please.*

They were on a lovely, tree-shaded country road. Calm and peaceful—that was the general impression. He couldn't even see much of any of the homes. On average, all the houses were on more than an acre of land. With its long winding driveways, manicured lawns and wooded backyards the area was unbelievably rustic. How could there be such evil in such a beautiful setting? Again he looked at Steve's mom. Her hands were covering her face.

Finally she spoke. "Oh God!" She did not uncover her face. "I can't believe we are having this conversation." She paused, removed her hands, and turned to face Greg. She gave him a rueful smile. "You sound like an adult. You're only sixteen, yet you sound like an adult."

Greg shook his head. "I'm old enough to know," he insisted

She exhaled loudly. "I feel I've ruined your childhood. And all because of my stupidity."

"Anybody can make a mistake," Greg told her seriously. "You shouldn't have to spend the rest of your life paying for it."

Again she was silent. Then she sighed again. "I should be the one saying that."

"Please Mom."

It was her turn to stare out the window. In a soft reflective voice she finally spoke. "I don't believe you are Daniel's son. But I have no proof."

"What do you mean?" Greg asked in quiet shock.

"Daniel and Harold were best friends.... A... a month after Harold and I got engaged, we were at a party. The three of us.... We all got drunk.... Oh God." She paused, exhaled again, loudly. "Steve... I really don't...."

"You can't stop now. Please," Greg pleaded. "Nothing you say will shock me. And I swear I'm not going to judge you," he promised rashly.

She was silent. He stared at her, willing her to continue. Her face was turned away. She took a tissue and dabbed at her eyes, but her eye makeup was already ruined. The tissue only made it worse.

"I'm going to have to do it all over again," she said with a nervous laugh as she wiped at her eyes.

Greg nodded. He was still hopeful.

Finally, after a long pause, she continued. "I... I don't remember a thing about that night. But... but... nine months later I had you."

Another long pause followed. Greg was about to give up on hearing more when she resumed.

"Harold... Harold never once hinted that there was any doubt about you being his son. *Never.* We got married shortly after the party.... He loved you. After... after he died, Daniel came to me with... with proof that he is your father. I... I... I still can't believe it." She covered her face with her hands again.

"What kind of proof?" Greg asked quietly. He was trying to hide his shock. *Steve will die. He'll just die. I'll never be able to tell him this!*

She was silent.

"Mom," he pleaded.

She took another tissue. "He showed me a copy

of a test Harold had done. The results said Harold was infertile."

"What?" this time Greg did not hide his shock.

"I still don't believe it," she whispered.

"Did you actually see the test results?"

"Yes," she nodded vigorously. "Yes. He said he and Harold both had the test done for a lark but Harold never bothered getting his results."

Greg was a bit reluctant to question her further—the shock of her revelation still lingered—but he needed more information. He thought furiously. What if Mr. Pierce was lying? The problem would then be to prove the lie. But how? He turned to her. "Do you still have a copy of the test results?"

"No. I think… I must have shredded it immediately."

"Do you remember anything about the test? Like the doctor's name, or the place where it was done?"

She looked puzzled. "No. Why?"

"I would love to track it down."

"How would that help?"

"Well, the copy he showed you could have been a fake."

"No. It was real. It looked real and was on a letterhead. And it was Harold's doctor."

"Then you *do* remember the name of the doctor."

"I could look that up. But would they have the records after sixteen years?"

"We could find out. Do you want me to try?"

"How?"

"By computer."

"Yes. Please try." She looked at him with new hope.

Since he was a little nervous about raising her hopes, he decided to steer the conversation back to something sure to upset her again.... her husband.

"Is that how he is blackmailing you?"

She pinched the bridge of her nose, and once again looked away. "It was such a shock... Harold's parents... I couldn't tell anyone.... Then... then Daniel said.... He wanted custody of you. He said he was planning to tell Harold, but of course Harold died before... I didn't want to fight a bitter custody battle with him. I was so afraid of losing you." Her head was down. She wrapped her arms around her body. "When he suggested we get married it seemed like the best plan...."

She gave a sudden bitter laugh. "Everything went well at first. We had known each other for years. I thought I knew him. The first time he got mad and hit me you were about two. I ran upstairs, grabbed you and packed my bags. Then I tried to leave. That is when he explained exactly what I had done by not telling anyone Harold was infertile."

"Harold left you a lot of money," Greg guessed.

She nodded. "God help me but I didn't want to go to jail for fraud and misrepresenting the facts or whatever else he said I had done. I would also have lost you too, and I couldn't bear that."

The enormity of her love for her son stunned Greg. Everything she had done, including putting up with her husband's abuse, was because she wanted to help her son. Greg didn't know what to say, "Oh, Mom."

Her laugh was again shaky. "He's not always violent, only when he is crossed. And it doesn't happen often."

Greg gave her an incredulous stare. "How can you still excuse him?"

"Either that or go crazy," she said wearily, as she leaned back again.

He abruptly reached for her, hugging her fiercely.

"Oh Steve. Oh Steve. God help me. Whether you are his son or not, I love you. You are mine." She took a couple of deep breaths. "But deep down, I really don't think you are his son. You have nothing for him. Nothing. I used to look and look for signs.... God help me. I even thought once of asking him to take a paternity test but I lost my nerve. God knows what he would do."

"It's alright, Mom. It's alright." Greg said, as he patted her comfortingly. But he wondered how Steve would have reacted. How *he* should be reacting. Certainly not so calm.... But what else could he do? It wouldn't help either of them if he panicked or pretended a deep hurt now. He continued patting her until she recovered.

She finally pulled away. Placing a hand on both of his shoulders she looked him squarely in the face. "I'm proud of you, you know. I couldn't wish for a better son."

For the first time in his life Greg knew what it was like to blush. As a black person, his face probably would have heated up, but he would have only felt hot. No one, besides himself, would have realized his embarrassment. But he was white. As his face heated, Greg was mortified. He ducked his head.

Mrs. Pierce laughed. It was her first real laugh since starting the car. "Now that I have ruined your day, what happens next?"

Greg grinned tentatively, relieved that she could

still laugh; relieved that the tension build-up was gone. "I'm okay. Sort of shocked, but okay. And I'm glad you told me. It's not half as bad as what I was thinking." He lied convincingly.

She gave him a squeeze. "Are you sure you will be okay?"

"I'm sure. Could you write me a note saying you know I'm late?"

With a smile and nod she complied. "That's not a problem."

A few minutes later Greg waved as he stepped out of the car. He would shelf this entire problem until later, he decided. Right now he had to deal with Tony Manelli.

Chapter Ten

"Morning," Steve said as he got into the back seat of Mr. Brent's Toyota. He was preoccupied as he mulled over his stepfather's behavior. *At least Mom seemed alright. But I should be there!*

He bitterly resented not being there for her and worried that Greg was too impulsive. Greg's behavior could just end up hurting his mother more. They had to change back—and soon. He came in shortly after eight last night. Although he didn't have a cell phone, he'd been smart enough to stop at a store and call to say he would be late, but still, he knew his excuse was a bit lame. The first part of his explanation, that he had asked Ray's aunt to drop him off at the library, was true. But the rest—forgetting the time—was definitely not. And while he had fooled Greg's mother, Germain was not impressed, and had in fact warned Steve that he knew Steve was lying. More than likely, Germain was planning some form of blackmail. It was one problem after another. He sighed and looked up in time to see Mr. Brent watching him through the rearview mirror. That man saw too much, Steve thought ruefully. In any other situation he would have liked him but as things stood this was no time to daydream.

Sure enough, Mr. Brent addressed the next question to him, "So what happened with Germain? Didn't he want a ride?"

"He said he promised to meet up with some friends," Steve said. Mr. Brent had offered to take both he and Germain each morning until his arm healed.

Ray, seated in the front, swiveled around. "I know the group he hangs out with. None of them is helping him."

You're right, Steve thought. Yesterday he saw the group that Germain considered his friends and they were all heading nowhere fast. Rather than get drawn into a discussion about Germain, he changed the subject. He, Ray and another friend of Ray's were planning to go out to the movies. They needed to decide on a day convenient to all of them.

The discussion lasted until Mr. Brent reached the school. *That takes care of another evening,* Steve thought as Mr. Brent dropped them off. He reluctantly got out of the car. There wasn't much he could do about his situation. It didn't even make sense worrying.

"Thanks Mr. Brent," he said as he grabbed his backpack.

"No problem, Greg."

Steve nodded, then started towards the school buildings with Ray. Although they were in the same homeroom, today he and Ray had only two other classes together—health and gym—which were fourth and sixth periods. Steve now followed Ray to their homeroom. Even after a full day of school, he was still uncomfortable around so many blacks. Yesterday he had been too scared to take in much. Today he compared the visual images that Greg had given him with the real thing. These buildings were a far cry from the country setting he was used to. The school was huge. Twice the size of his school, it consisted of four stories of red brick. It had been planned with each floor representing a year, with the freshmen year on the top floor. As sophomores, their homerooms and the bulk of their classes were on the third floor.

Steve did not attempt to fight the subconscious disdain he felt for this school. Coming from a wealthy suburb, his comparisons were naturally negative. As he saw things, he could well have dropped into another country. Even the language was different. English yes, but.... Then there was the culture here. Perhaps because there just wasn't a large black population at his school to form separate black groups versus white groups, the few blacks naturally socialized with the whites. They partied together, went to each other's houses.... Here the blacks joined blacks-only groups, whites formed whites-only groups and the Hispanics and Asians also had their own cliques. The entire school was segregated.

He was so intent on his comparisons that he spoke his thoughts aloud. "It would make more sense to have separate schools. This forced integration makes no sense."

Ray gave him a sharp glance. "What do you mean?" he asked pointedly.

Steve hesitated. He gave Ray a quick look, then decided to continue. "Well, the blacks only socialize with the blacks and the whites only socialize with the whites. Hispanics at least seem to mix a little. They can go either way. But it shouldn't be like that."

"Tell me about it," Ray said bitterly. "And I fit in nowhere."

Steve didn't want to say it but Ray was right. Ray obviously took after his mother's side of the family. He had dark blond curls, hazel eyes and an olive complexion. His features were.... Well they weren't exactly white, but neither were they black. He was definitely the 'other' category found on all official forms.

"But you have friends," he began tentatively "What I mean is...."

"Sure, I have white friends and black friends here at the school but we don't really do much together outside of school. Take that guy over there." He pointed to a white student in his class. "We use to study together all the time. But just last year, he had a big party at his house and invited all the white kids in the class, but not one black. That's how it's always been. Most of the blacks and Hispanics live on the south side of the town and the whites live on the north. Once we leave school it's a black, Hispanic or white world."

Steve was beginning to understand. It wasn't that the whites were unfriendly. They weren't. It was just that here he was regarded as a black classmate rather than as a classmate. It was so frustrating! And he couldn't even call it racism because the blacks did the same thing. That was why Ray had so much difficulty fitting in. They didn't really want him in either group.

When Steve did not respond, Ray turned to him. "It's true if you think about it."

"You're right," Steve said thoughtfully. He wondered what Ray would say if he confided in him—told him that he and Greg had switched. No. Ray would never believe him. No one would. But he wasn't sure how much longer he would be able to live like this. Maybe it would be different if he had been born black. Then he would have grown up accepting things the way they were. But now.... This switch and trying to deal with this racial thing was driving him crazy.

"I would hate to live...." he paused, shocked at what he almost revealed. He rushed quickly into speech, "What I really mean is I don't see why I shouldn't join a white group.... Why can't we just forget about racial groups?"

Ray did not notice his slip. "Well, number one, the blacks would call you a traitor. They would never let up ragging you. Then the whites may sort of tolerate you while here at school but you wouldn't really be a part of their lives. Not out of school anyway. Forget it. You will never change the world."

"I think blacks are deliberately resisting integration."

Ray stared. "What do you mean?"

"They feel they will lose something if they socialize with whites."

"That's nonsense!"

"It isn't if you think about it. They cling together and try to force all other blacks to stay within the group. Anyone trying to leave is branded a traitor to the cause."

"What cause? Are you crazy? You're acting as if you aren't black." Ray was still staring at him. "If blacks wanted to remain separate, they would never have fought so hard for integration."

"Alright, alright." But Steve was sure he was right— after all, he was now able to compare both sides. He realized, however, that if he continued this argument Ray would soon suspect something. "You're probably right," he said, reluctantly. "Look. Let's just drop the argument, okay?"

Ray wasn't yet willing to let go. "Blacks cling together because the whites don't really want to socialize with them. So the blacks have their own social groups."

"But in school—"

Ray interrupted. "You grew up in this school. You saw how it was. We all mixed during elementary school. Then in middle school the changes started. One or two people may resist, but for the most part you would see the start of distinct groups—all white, all Hispanic or all black. If you didn't conform—regardless of your race—you would be shut out. You notice the few Asian kids stick together too."

"It doesn't happen like this in all schools," Steve insisted.

"How do you know? You've never been to any other school."

Steve paused. He could hardly admit that he had. Then inspiration struck. "If it did, your parents would never have met and got married."

Ray immediately turned away.

Steve was appalled at what he had just said. "Ray... I didn't mean to bring that up. I'm sorry." In his eagerness to prove his point he had forgotten Ray's mother's death.

"It's alright." Ray's head was bent. "I...." He stopped. "I was being an idiot anyway. It's time I got over it. I know Mom would be mad if she was alive and seeing how I'm acting."

Steve said nothing. He did not want to make things worse. But he was also curious. This was the first time Ray had volunteered any information on his mother.

They continued walking towards their lockers. Ray did not speak for a long while. Finally, just when Steve had given up on him, he haltingly continued, "You're probably right. 'Cause Dad always said he and Mom first met in school. They kept in touch with each other even through college." He stopped abruptly and stared at Steve. "Is that why you're suddenly talking to me? Because you feel we shouldn't keep separate groups?"

"No!" Steve was indignant. He turned to face Ray. "Don't be a moron, Ray. I'm not talking to you just to prove a point."

Ray gave him a slight grin. "Never mind me. I...." He made lightning-quick subject change. "I promised Dad I would get my grades up. I've been fooling around for the past year-and-a-half so now I'm going to have to work extra hard."

Steve nodded. He accepted the change of subject but unlike Ray, he was unable to rapidly move on to a new topic. And Ray clearly did not want to confide further.

"I have to get something from my locker," Ray jerked his head in the direction of his locker.

"Okay. Meet you for English," Steve said as the two separated.

Their lockers were in different areas of the hallway. Steve watched him go. *I'll have to explain this to Greg.* He just hoped Greg would feel the same way about things. It would be awful if Greg came back and shunned Ray. Especially now that Ray was trying to get over his mother's death. *This system isn't right. I shouldn't be the only one to notice the problems. Why don't the teachers do something? They see how the kids are acting. They must have seen the slow change as kids moved from elementary, to middle, to high school. Why didn't they do something?* Remembering Greg's words about blacks and self-esteem, Steve figured fear probably played a major role in the separation of the races at school—fear of not being accepted and fear of being alone. Each group wanted company—a safe group to hang out with. They found that with people who looked like themselves and since no one pushed the issue, they looked no further.

Steve just hoped his talk hadn't scared away his one and only friend. They didn't get a chance to talk during English and afterwards they separated for bio. Steve hurried into the class a few minutes late. He was still learning to find his way around and had twice got lost.

Mr. Stevens, the bio teacher, was discussing the last test papers.

"I am going to go over these answers with you before giving back the papers," Mr. Stevens said, as he went to the head of the class.

As he pulled out his notes, Steve frowned over the work. These classes just were not challenging. It was something that he had forgotten to ask Greg about. They were so similar that he had assumed that Greg was also an honor student. But now he had his doubts.

Steve spent a boring twenty minutes as the teacher discussed the last test. Finally, finally, Mr. Stevens returned the last test papers.

Steve looked at the grade and almost exclaimed aloud. The work was graded C. He quickly flipped through the paper, getting angrier by the minute. *How dumb can you get?* He angrily picked out Greg's errors. *Stupid! Stupid!*

Stupid! Then another thought hit. *Greg is going to mess up my grades!* For his entire life he had never got less than an 'A' on any test. He was extraordinarily proud of his grades. A full scholarship was his goal. Maybe even to Yale, Harvard or Princeton. No way did he want to be forever dependant on his stepfather. If Greg lowered his grades, he would.... Steve seethed. Why had he assumed that he and Greg had similar abilities? *He should have known better than to expect a black....*

He stopped abruptly. A month, a week, even a few days ago perhaps he would have completed the thought. Now a feeling of shame caused his face to heat up as he recognized how stereotypical such thoughts were. *But damn it! Are there any class tests pending? Oh no! Next week is the SAT! Maybe he could contact Greg during the test and work with him.* He couldn't afford to have Greg mess up. That's what Greg's mother meant when he first spoke to her on Thursday. Her comment about grades was meaningless then. Now he knew. Steve scowled as another thought occurred. *How in the world am I going to approach Greg?* Greg might well refuse his help. *Damn! Damn!*

Mr. Stevens came by his desk. "I expect to see an improvement on your next test," he warned.

"You sure will," Steve promised fervently.

"Good. I'm glad you decided to take my advice." Mr. Steven was clearly pleased.

What advice? Steve was blank. He gave a weak smile. Fortunately for him, Mr. Stevens moved on.

As he left the room, he was still puzzling over Greg's unexpectedly low grades and trying to figure out a way of keeping his grades the same. He hurried to the next subject, math. He remembered the class from yesterday. The class was boring, the work painfully easy. No. Something was not right! Steve began reflecting on past conversations with Greg. Had they ever mentioned grades? Not that he recalled. But the more he thought about it, the more he realized that something was definitely wrong. He had spent boring hours exploring Greg's room, reading his books and rummaging through his things. They were just too similar to have such different abilities.

He was so deep in thought as he headed to health and to meet up with Ray that Germain had to call twice before he finally realized he was being called. Or it could be that he still wasn't used to responding to the name Greg. Steve stopped and waited for Germain to catch up.

"Are you getting a ride this evening?"

"Yes. But you have basketball, don't you?"

"No. Well.... Listen I've arranged a ride for us."

"What are you talking about?" Steve was puzzled. Besides, from what Greg had told him, Germain usually pretended that the two of them were not even related, much less brothers.

"Where will you be?"

"I can't just back out from going with Ray's aunt," Steve said. He could not hide his curiosity, however. "What's up?"

"It's Dad. I've arranged for him to pick us up."

Steve had totally forgotten his promise. "I... I...."

"You promised." Germain gave him an aggressive stare.

"I expected you to tell me first. You can't just arrange something like this."

"Damn it, Greg. You promised. You aren't going to back out of this," Germain hissed.

"I'm not backing out. But you shouldn't have arranged this without telling me."

"What was there to tell?"

"You know what I'm talking about."

"You don't really mean to meet him, do you? You are just making excuses and more excuses."

"I'm not making excuses."

Germain just glared. "Will you come?"

"I...."

"I hate you!" In a flare of temper Germain abruptly pushed Steve, violently, into the wall.

On any other occasion, Steve would not have fallen. But his left hand was still in the cast, and his ribs were strapped. He tottered for a second, banged into the wall, then lost his balance.

"Aaah," Steve cried, flailing desperately. It was hopeless. He crashed to the ground. Pain shot up his arm. White-hot pain. He gasped. Steve fought nausea as the pain rippled throughout his chest.

< "Steve! Steve! What the hell happened?"> Greg sounded panicky, his voice reflecting the pain Steve was feeling. < "Shit! My arm! My chest!">

Steve moaned. Or was it Greg? He was literally unable to respond to Greg's panic. He tried a deep breath, but stopped abruptly as that only increased his pain. He held his breath—terrified to breathe! Finally, unable to hold it any longer, he took a quick shallow breath—bearable, just bearable. He tried a few more shallow breaths and then cautiously opened his eyes. Germain was staring at him, ashen-faced and terrified. As soon as he saw Steve's eyes open he backed away, slowly at first then with increasing speed.

"I'll get help."

"Greg! Holy Shit! What happened?" Ray was rushing towards him.

Ray bent to help him up.

"No!" Steve cried. He was afraid any movement would increase his pain. The sharp pain in his chest was beginning to recede. It was still there, but as long as he took only shallow breaths it was just a dull throb. His left arm was another story. With every heartbeat pulsating pain radiated up his arm. Worse, he had landed on his left side. His left upper arm rested on the floor, supporting most of his weight. Cautiously, he eased down further, to lie flat on his back. At least now the floor supported his arm.

"Germain says the nurse is coming," Ray reassured him.

"Okay," Steve muttered, closing his eyes. A crowd was gathering, and he began sweating. He could hear their voices and now he was feeling too embarrassed to face them. He hadn't been able to respond to Greg before; now he gave a mental call.

< "Greg?">

< "I think I'll live,"> Greg muttered. < "Just.">

< "Me too,"> Steve gave a shaky mental grin.

< "What happened?">

< "I... fell."> Steve said after a slight pause. He kept a tight rein on his thoughts, reluctant to let Greg know that Germain had pushed him. Besides, he was sure Germain really hadn't meant to hurt him.

Greg was silent for a moment, then sent Steve a blast of pure rage. < "You fell! Do you know what you just did?"> He shouted. < "I was in the middle of global and suddenly I cried out and keeled over, clutching my arm and chest and moaning. Now I have nothing to show for it. No cut. No bruise. Nothing! And everyone is bending over me. They have even sent for the nurse. I'll never live this down. Never!">

< "Well. A nurse is coming here too,"> Steve pointed out.

< "At least you have a reason for your pain. You have a cracked rib and a cast on."> He stopped suddenly. < "Oh, no!">

< "What?"
Steve responded to the sudden note of pure panic.

< "The nurse wants me to unbutton my shirt. I can't. The marks. I can't open my shirt. The whip marks.">

< "I'll get up,"> Steve said desperately. No one must see those marks! He opened his eyes, this time ignoring the crowd of students, and tried focusing on Ray, who was bending over him with a worried frown. "Help me up, Ray. Help me up."

"Let's wait for the nurse," Ray said soothingly. "She's coming."

"No. No! Help me up!" Steve tried to move but another sharp pain ripped through his chest. A groan escaped.

< "Steve! Don't move!"> Greg screamed. < "I'll get up. You stay still. If you aren't in pain, I won't be. Stay still!">

Steve froze. Closing his eyes, he tried concentrating

on willing his pain away. If Greg went to the nurse's office and was examined, they would see a mess of healed and healing welts on his arm and back. That must not happen.

The nurse was bending over him. "Greg? Greg, can you speak? Where does it hurt?"

Steve took a quick breath. "My chest, my arm," he gasped out. He did not open his eyes. The nurse touched his chest. "I can't move," he cried out in panic, deathly afraid she would try to lift him.

"Don't worry," she said. "I'm not going to move you. I'm going to call an ambulance. I think you may have cracked another rib. And your arm definitely needs another cast. We aren't going to touch you until they come." Steve risked opening his eyes again. Ray and some other students were picking up his scattered books.

"I'll give them to Germain to take home," Ray said.

Steve gave a brief nod.

"What happened?" the nurse asked.

"I fell," Steve said. The lie came easier. "I tripped and fell."

The nurse accepted his explanation without question. "You have to be more careful, unless your plan is to spend more time in the hospital than here at school."

Steve gave her a weak grin. He closed his eyes again, to concentrate on Greg, but the ambulance had arrived.

Despite the paramedics' care, pain ripped throughout his chest again as he was lifted onto a stretcher. Steve bit down hard on his lips to stop himself from crying out. The metallic taste of blood in his mouth told him he was only inflicting more damage on himself. He stopped. He tried reaching Greg again, but couldn't do that while trying to keep the pain at bay. He was terrified! And his imagination wasn't helping any. What was happening with Greg? Had the nurse seen anything? Would she contact police? *I can't take this stress! Please, oh please don't let the nurse see Greg's welts!*

Chapter Eleven

Greg was sweating. Much as he tried, he couldn't separate himself from Steve's pain. And the nurse was now bending over him.

"Steve, what happened? Where exactly does it hurt?"

Greg couldn't answer. The other students were eager to pick up the slack.

"He just fell, screaming."

"It's his arm."

"His chest, too."

"Do you think he ruptured his appendix?"

Greg tried to block out the babble. *Concentrate. Concentrate. I have to block out Steve!*

The nurse tried to raise his shirt.

"No! No! Please. I'll be fine in a minute," he gasped. He took a deep breath, but as with Steve, that was the worst thing he could possibly have done. He gasped.

"Steve, if you can't tell me what's wrong, I'll have to call the ambulance. Where does it hurt? What happened?"

"I just need a minute," Greg gasped.

"Are you hurt?"

"No."

"He's faking," someone called out.

Greg recognized the voice—Tony Manelli. This was all he needed. Tony had been needling him ever since he stepped into the building this morning. The kid was obviously an unchecked bully and Greg was waiting for Tony to actually touch him physically. If that happened, Mr. Pierce could kiss the Manelli account goodbye.

What made Greg mad was he had started out the day with good intentions. He truly meant to try making it up with Tony—for Steve's Mom's sake only. His good intentions had lasted through the first period and exactly ten minutes into second period. That's when it finally clicked that the other students, who ignored him during first period, were now giving him muffled smirks or looking at him, grinning, then looking away. He tried to ignore them. Something was up—but what? Then he was called to the front of the class by the teacher. It was his turn to work out the math problem. As he stood up, the class broke out in titters. It became outright laughter as he turned his back to the class and started writing on the chalkboard.

"Quiet!" the teacher bellowed sharply. As he turned to Greg, his expression and voice changed to one of exasperation. "What is this?"

The teacher reached for a paper stuck on Greg's back.

Greg turned and read the note. That's when his second blush—and in one day—occurred. He was positive even his toes were red.

'Smell me. I didn't wash or take a bath this morning,' the note said.

"This," the teacher said as he held up the note, "is

something I would expect of first or second-graders, not tenth-graders." He crumbled the note and chucked it into the waste bin, his expression one of disgust.

His actions in no way mollified Greg's embarrassment. *Tony!* He was livid! He directed a furious glare at Tony. *I'll get even. Just you wait.*

Unaware of his vow, Tony gave him a satisfied smile.

Greg gave him another cold look, determined to project some of his thoughts. Perhaps he succeeded, because Tony stopped smiling. The look he now gave Greg was one of defiance. *Yes, Tony definitely needs to be brought down a peg or two.* He turned back to the chalkboard, finished his problem, then returned to his seat.

As they were leaving the classroom, Tony caught up with him. "Guess who stuck the paper to your back?" he asked with a smirk.

Greg didn't answer.

"It was Jack." Tony's animosity was plain. "I told him to do it, and he did. You want to know why?"

Greg hitched his backpack higher on his shoulder and ignored Tony as he headed for the next class.

"Don't you want to know why no one is talking to you?" Like a tenacious insect, Tony was following him.

Greg stopped. "Why don't you get it all off your chest then get lost?" he said, as he turned to Tony.

Tony was still smirking. "I'm planning a cruise on the Hudson. Everyone in math and chemistry is invited—except you."

For a second Greg could only stare at Tony. Then his words sank in. He could not believe this. Tony was bribing the entire class. Bribing the class to ostracize him! Without a word, he turned to his other classmates. Most were on their way out the door—to the next class. The ones closest to Tony, those who had heard his words, avoided eye contact and hurried on. Paula shrugged and looked guilty but did not come towards him. He sought out Jack. Jack was almost at the end of the hallway. Brushing past Tony, he headed for his so-called friend, catching up with him just as the other boy entered the next class.

Greg caught Jack's arm, pulling him to a halt. "Is it true?"

Jack avoided his eyes. "I need to go." He tried pulling away.

Greg tightened his grip, forcing Jack to stay put. "What else did he bribe you with?"

"Just leave it, Steve. I warned you. Leave it." Jack pulled away.

Someone laughed. Greg turned around. Tony was just behind him, a complacent smile in place. Greg's mouth tightened. He said nothing as he walked into the next class.

Aleck came up to him "So what did you do to upset the Great Tony Manelli?"

"I walked away from his lunch table—in the middle of one of his best jokes."

"Good." Aleck laughed.

Greg looked at him curiously, "Aren't you going on the cruise?"

"Are you kidding? Tony never forgives or forgets unless you go groveling to him. Chris wasn't invited either." Aleck named three other students, then shook his head mournfully. "We all insulted or upset Tony at one time or another, so now we have to pay for our sins."

Greg suddenly grinned. "Let's form the Those Against Tony Fan Club."

"Good idea," Aleck gave a thoughtful nod. "T.A.T.F.C. No. That's not right. How about F.A.T.—Forever Against Tony. Sounds good."

It sounded so good, Greg spent the rest of global studies fantasizing about ways of getting back at Tony. Aleck, however, was serious. Greg saw him broach the subject with another student. *What have I started?* He had to avoid looking at Aleck to control his laughter. Maybe after class he would tell Aleck he'd just been kidding. *But it was such a good idea!*

"Steve!"

Greg's head jerked up as he realized the teacher was calling him. *I have to stop daydreaming.* The work was much more challenging than his recent classes. Not that he couldn't cope—he just had to work a bit harder rather than coast along during the classes. He remembered the challenge, and how much he really enjoyed it.

"Steve, I asked a question."

Greg sighed. He had no idea what the question was, much less the answer.

Mrs. Crew, the global studies teacher, gave him an irritated look. "Stand and tell the class..." she began.

That's when Greg felt as if his chest had exploded. Pain shot up his arm. He groaned—bending forward and clutching at his chest and arm.

Steve!

* * * *

Greg struggled for control as he now listened in growing anger to Tony's version of what happened.

"For some reason, he's faking it. He was fine until Mrs. Crew asked him a question," Tony explained to the nurse.

His classmates, like dutiful echoes, agreed. Since Greg could offer no other explanation he resigned himself to the worst, closed his eyes and checked in on Steve.

< "I'm feeling much better as long as I don't move,"> Steve said.

< "Where are you?">

< "In an ambulance.">

< "Let me know if they're going to do anything painful, okay?">

< "Sure.">

Greg opened his eyes and slowly pushed himself upright. "I'm alright now," he muttered. The pain was still there, but muted.

The nurse was still worried—her expression uneasy.

Mrs. Crew was clearly suspicious. "Steve, I hope this was not a planned disturbance," she said.

"It wasn't. I had a sharp stabbing pain in my side, but it's gone now."

She stared at him in silence, then looked to the nurse for guidance.

The nurse pursed her lips, then abruptly came to a decision. "I want you to come to my office and let me check you out."

"No. I mean.... I'm fine now," Greg protested.

"Come anyway."

Greg reluctantly walked with her to her office.

"Would you like me to call your mother?"

"No. I told you I am fine." Even as he said it, he felt another sharp stab of pain in his arm. *What's happening now! There is no way I can contact Steve with the nurse staring at me. She's already suspicious.*

Greg had thought she was suspicious because she believed he was faking. She soon disabused him of that theory.

"You're too pale and you're sweating. Something is not right. What?"

Greg took a quick breath. The pain in his chest was definitely coming back. *Not again! What the hell is happening?*

< "Greg?">

Greg couldn't answer him. He instead projected the scene, allowing Steve to see and hear what was happening. Then he turned to the nurse. "May I sit for a minute or so?"

"Would you prefer that I call your father?" the nurse asked, instead of replying.

"No!" Greg was horrified.

"Steve, since you refuse to let me examine you, I have to call one of your parents. Which one will it be?" She waved him to a seat as she took up the telephone. "Sit. Sit."

"Okay. You can call my mom," Greg muttered.

"Do you know her number?"

Greg gave her the cell phone number, knowing that Mrs. Pierce could be anywhere. As she started dialing, turning her attention away from him, he quickly contacted Steve.

< "What's happening with you?"> he asked.

< "Nothing. They're just transferring me to the

hospital. I should be pain free for a while, but later I'm going to have x-rays, then they'll see."›

‹ "Okay... okay. I can't talk now."› Greg, who had bent forward to contact Steve, now straightened to listen to the nurse.

"No," she was saying to Mrs. Pierce on the telephone. "I didn't examine him. He refused to remove his shirt. I have no idea what's wrong." She listened for a while then turned to Greg. "Your mother wants to talk with you."

Greg took the phone. "Hi."

"Steve, does this have anything to do with the conversation we had in the car this morning?" Mrs. Pierce asked worriedly.

"No. No. I just have this awful stabbing pain in my side." Knowing that the pain could get worse, depending on what they did to Steve in the hospital, he continued, "Could you pick me up? I'm really not feeling well."

"I'll be there in a little bit. The nurse said you could stay in her office. Will that be okay?"

"Fine, er... Mom. Do you want to speak to the nurse again?"

"No. Just tell her I'm on my way."

Greg hung up and relayed the message. The nurse then directed him to one of the beds where he was able to lie down—and not a minute too soon. He rolled on his right side, his back to her, and stuffed the pillow into his mouth to prevent crying out loud.

Seconds later Steve's voice came. ‹ "Greg, I'm sorry,"› he said with a gasp. ‹ "They're taking x-rays and the x-ray tech just moved my arm."›

< "Okay. Just tell them to hurry."> He tried switching positions but changed his mind as another sharp stab of pain hit. < "Your mother is going to pick me up.">

< "Did the nurse see anything?">

< "No. I didn't let her examine me.">

He felt Steve's sigh of relief as the other boy backed out.

Less then fifteen minutes later, however, Steve contacted him again.

< "Greg, they are going to put me to sleep. They have to reset my arm. Right now they are just waiting for your mom's permission. And they are already trying to contact her.">

< "When? Now?">

< "In a few minutes.">

Oh, no! Greg thoughts were panicky. *What if I still feel all of Steve's pain, even while Steve's unconscious? I'll never be able to bear it!*

< "Is my mom there yet?">

< "No. No. She said she'd be here soon.">

< "I'll try and delay them a bit—at least until you can get home."> It was obvious Steve had read Greg's panicky thoughts.

< "Warn me before they start,"> Greg said. He was sweating already, his entire body tensing, readying itself for the pain. Then he heard Mrs. Pierce. *Thank God.*

< "She's here.">

< "Good.">

Greg turned slowly, and stood as Mrs. Pierce entered the office.

She was extremely worried. "What happened? Are

you okay now?"

"Not really," Greg said with a weak grin. "Could we go now? I just need to lie down."

"You may want to consider getting him to a doctor if the pain continues," the nurse suggested. "He now says it's his stomach. But earlier on he was holding his chest and arm. You might want to check those areas as well."

"I will. I will," she said as she signed him out.

Greg was halfway to the door when she caught up with him.

"Steve, are you sure it's nothing?"

"I'm positive. I really need to lie down. Can we hurry?"

Along the way to the car she had to hurry to keep up with Greg's long strides and kept giving him worried looks, although she said nothing.

In the car she chewed on her lips as she turned to look at him. Greg was reclining in his seat, his eyes half closed.

"Steve?"

"I'm fine."

"No, you're not. And I can't take you to a doctor."

"Can we just get home?" Greg asked desperately. He could not reassure her. He just wanted to get home as fast as possible just in case he continued feeling Steve's pain while the doctors set his fracture.

Mrs. Pierce started the car. School was only ten minutes from home. Five minutes into the journey Steve contacted him

< "Greg, I'm sorry. They are going to start now.">

Greg clenched his teeth. He was too scared to reply.

Chapter Twelve

Slowly, Steve opened his eyes. He blinked in confusion as he tried to remember what had happened.

"Greg?"

He turned, responding to the voice if not the name.

"Oh. Thank God you are alright." Mrs. Martin was staring down at him mistily.

Steve gave her a shaky smile.

"Your teacher told me what happened. Oh Greg. You have to be more careful or that arm will never heal."

He gave a drowsy nod. What he really needed to do was contact Greg, but his mind was too sluggish to concentrate. He was aware that Greg's mother stayed for a while—he was not aware when she left.

Later, Greg's insistent calls woke him.

Steve jerked awake in a panic. *Oh my God! Greg! What if they took Greg to the hospital? What if...?*

< "I'm fine. Nothing happened">

Steve sent up a silent prayer. His heart stopped racing. < "How did you manage?">

< "I didn't have to do a thing. Nothing happened.">
Greg grinned. < "It seems I only feel your pain if you're awake and can feel it too. Maybe when we are awake, we

unconsciously send feelings or pain.">

< "So you didn't feel anything when I had the surgery?"> Steve did not mask his amazement.

< "Not a thing! As soon as they put you to sleep the pain left me.">

< "Good!">

< "Yeah, I know."> Greg agreed fervently. < "Tell me about it. I was sweating.">

Steve grinned; he felt enormously relieved. He continued teasingly, < "I was afraid I'd wake up to find you in some mental institution or something.">

< "Huh! We may yet end up there, so don't laugh.">

Steve refused to get depressed. He laughed, < "Nope. I think we just passed our worst test.">

< "We already failed our worst test,"> Greg objected.

Steve was silent for a minute as he absorbed Greg's change of mood. < "Okay, what gives?"> Resignation was already setting in. Something was definitely wrong.

< "He thinks I'm on drugs."> Greg finally admitted.

< "Drugs!"> Steve did not hide his shock. < "Why drugs?">

Greg gave the mental equivalent of a shrug. < "Damned if I know. He thinks I act different, I guess.">

< "Different! Greg I told you....">

< "Well, we are different!"> Greg interrupted. < "What do you expect me to do? Keep my mouth shut and my head down? Even identical twins are different and we sure aren't identical.">

< "Okay. Okay. So what did he do? Or what did you do?">

< "I didn't do anything. He called the school and

had them search my locker. I can just imagine what the other kids are saying now.">

< "Hell!">

< "Yeah!">

< "Well at least they didn't find anything in the locker.">

< "But he's still suspicious. And he's not letting up. He had your Mom search your room and I'm grounded for the week.">

More complications; it never ends. Steve rubbed his temple. He had the beginnings of a tension headache. Then another thought occurred.

< "Greg, I'm beginning to get a headache. How do you feel?">

< "I have it too. I thought it was just me. This computer is driving me crazy.">

< "Computer?"> Steve was distracted from his original idea. < "What are you talking about?">

Greg sighed.

Steve sensed that Greg had slipped up by mentioning the computer. Greg was now clearly reluctant to talk. < "Greg?"> he asked impatiently.

< "A hunch. I was just working on a hunch. Something your mother said. I was trying to find more information on the computer but so far I haven't come up with anything.">

< "What are you talking about?"> Steve was curiously hurt that his mother had obviously confided in Greg, something she had never done with him.

Greg must have sensed his hurt because he quickly explained. < "It's not much. She just volunteered something.

I guess I pushed her a bit,"> he added.

< "And then you wonder why HE thinks you're different,"> Steve said bitterly.

Greg was silent.

< "Well, what did she tell you?"> Steve asked, after it became obvious Greg was not going to volunteer any further information.

< "She gave me some information on your dad."> Greg was speaking slowly and with obvious misgivings. < "I was trying to check it out. But he's not in the system.">

< "What information?"> When Greg didn't answer, he lost his temper. < "Why you... you.... You... you're still trying to prove my mother is a liar."> Steve slammed his good arm down on the bed in frustration. < "I HATE this!">

* * * *

Steve raged in helpless fury against fate. *Why? Why? Why did this have to happen to me!* The worst of it was he was terrified that Greg might be right. *What will I do then? Return and accept as a father a man who beat his wife? I can't! I just can't!*

< "Steve that's not true. I wasn't trying to prove that your mother is a liar. I was trying to prove the opposite. I was trying to prove....">

< "Will you get the hell out of my mind?"> Steve screamed.

Greg exited—abruptly and completely.

Steve took a deep breath *Damn! Damn! Damn!* He now had a massive headache and he had just blown the perfect opportunity to test whether they both felt the same pain and to try controlling it. Lowering the bed, he shifted slightly to a more comfortable position, closed his eyes, and tried to relax. His peace did not last long.

"Hi Greg."

Ray and his dad had entered the room.

"This is becoming a bad habit." Mr. Brent greeted him.

"Yeah I know."

"So how are you?" Mr. Brent drew a chair up.

Depressed, suicidal—those were his first dramatic thoughts. He gave a weak grin and said, "I'm not in any real pain. I think I must be stuffed full of drugs."

"God forbid," Mr. Brent smiled.

Ray plopped down on the only other chair in the room. "Greg, I can't believe you did this to yourself."

"I can't believe it either," Steve muttered.

"Cheer up," Ray teased. "It could have been your other arm."

Steve scowled.

Mr. Brent interrupted before the two could really get to each other.

"Do you know that Germain went home with your father?"

Hell! Steve thought. *What a mess.* "Yes," he admitted haltingly. "I knew he was going."

"Does your mother know about Germain meeting with your father?"

"Know?" Steve stalled.

"Don't act cute, Greg," Mr. Brent said impatiently. "Does your mother know?" he repeated.

When Steve still didn't answer Mr. Brent continued.

"My sister's husband is a good friend of your father. You may have met them, Amanda and Ian Connelly?"

If Greg had met them, Steve didn't know anything about it. But he could hardly confess that.

"I don't know if my mother knows," he reluctantly answered the first question. "He has visitation rights. But we sort of agreed not to see him. And he didn't insist. Then Germain decided to see him," Steve didn't care how confusing his explanation was sounding. He continued to mumble. "Gr...." *Oh Great! I almost said 'Greg.'* Now he was really getting rattled. "I don't want her to know," he continued in a louder voice. He reluctantly told them about his parents' break up, deciding to do so only because he suspected Mr. Brent already knew about it.

"Have you spoken to Germain?"

"Hundreds of times," he muttered. "Not that it made any difference."

"You need to speak with your mother."

"Yes...." Steve knew that Greg would definitely agree with that.

Mr. Brent nodded. "Good." He changed the subject. "How long are they going to keep you here, Greg?"

"I didn't get a chance to ask. This is the first time I've been fully awake. What time is it anyway?"

"Three," Ray said.

"Three! I slept through the entire day!"

They stayed and chatted a bit but Steve was clearly preoccupied so they soon left. Minutes later Greg's mother and Germain walked in.

Germain looked uncomfortable. Steve watched him, trying to figure out exactly what was wrong but Greg's mother soon distracted him with her attention.

He reassured her for the hundredth time that he was okay and not in any pain. Not that it made any difference. Besides he really didn't mind; her care soothed him. She really was a very nice lady. Nice but.... He searched for the right word. It wasn't that she did not care about her son's welfare. She did. But she just seemed unaware of the troubles lurking around her.

If he had come home at eight o'clock, his parents would have had a fit. Just look at the hard time they gave Greg when he got in at seven. Yet here Mrs. Martin accepted his explanation without question.

After thinking about it for a while Steve realized that she treated Greg and Germain like adults and expected them to make adult decisions. Maybe it was because as virtually a single mother, she was forced to rely on their help and leave them on their own even when they were young. Whatever the reason, she seemed to have little or no control over either of her boys.

He frowned again as he thought of Greg and the upheavals being created in his family. Greg was decidedly too interfering. Funny how he was unable to solve his family's problems yet he was bent on meddling with Steve's family.

"Are you in pain again?" Greg's mother asked, as she noticed his frown.

"Only a slight headache," Steve said. He could hardly confide his thoughts.

"I'll see if I can get a nurse to get you something for it." She started to turn away.

"It's not bad, Mom," Steve protested.

"Mom, you're babying him. There is nothing much wrong with him."

Mrs. Martin turned a stern face at Germain. "I think it's about time I babied Greg." She declared firmly. "He has always acted so much older than his years that I keep forgetting he's only sixteen." Turning back to Steve, she said, "I'll get you something. I'll be right back." She left the room.

"What did Dad say?" he asked Germain as soon as they were alone.

Germain gave him a hard stare. "Why should I tell you? You aren't really interested." He glared at Steve. "You were only pretending to have a headache, weren't you? Just to get petted and to get Mom out of the room."

"I have a headache, I'm not lying." It was the truth. In fact, it was steadily getting worse—a massive tension headache.

"Yeah. Right." Germain clearly did not believe him.

Steve shrugged and turned away. Why should he care one way or another?

Mrs. Martin came back into the room with a nurse in tow. The nurse was very friendly and helpful but after checking his charts refused to give him any more medication. She and Mrs. Martin spent the next few minutes discussing Steve as if he wasn't even there. Steve began feeling uncomfortable. Great! Next they were going to start discussing his bowels! The only useful bit of information he got was that he was running a fever so they couldn't discharge him tonight. If the fever went down, he would be out by tomorrow morning. He was positively relieved when Mrs. Martin finally allowed the nurse to leave.

For a minute there was silence. Germain had been sulking and was still standing and staring out the window.

Mrs. Martin glanced from him to Steve then back to Germain.

"Okay. What's wrong between the two of you now?"

Germain just scowled harder. Steve hesitated, then abruptly decided to take the plunge. It was now or never and he was too stressed to think up a subtle way of introducing the topic.

"Mom, is it true that you were seeing another man while Dad was away at sea?"

Germain jerked around in horror. Mrs. Martin gave him a shocked stare.

"What?" She finally found her voice to ask.

"Mom," Steve took a deep breath. He wanted to clutch his head. He felt he now knew what a migraine was. "Mom, we need to know. We've been hearing all these rumors. We really need to know. Why was he—Dad—so mad? Why can't you tell us what happened?"

She groped for a chair and sank down without speaking.

"Mom?" Steve asked. He took a quick look at Germain. Germain was nervously licking his lips.

"What did he say?"

They did not need to ask who 'he' was.

Germain answered. "Dad said.... Well I heard him talking with someone. So I got the whole story." His tone was truculent.

"What did he say?" Mrs. Martin was insistent.

Germain had the grace to look shamefaced. He scuffed the toe of his sneaker on the tile floor and remained stubbornly silent.

Steve filled in the breech. He repeated what Germain had told him, but tried for a neutral tone.

Mrs. Martin listened in silence. At the end she got up and stood, staring out the window.

"It's not true," she did not turn to them as she spoke. "The worst of it is it's all lies. Unfortunately, the only person who can back up my side of the story is dead."

"They had pictures," Germain was clearly skeptical.

"Joe was dying. I knew him long before I met your father and bumped into him again one day. It was just by accident. We met again a few times after that. I knew he had a brain tumor. He just wanted to spend his last days enjoying himself. He had no children—no wife. So he took out most of his savings and decided to splurge. I was not the only one he invited on his trips. Whoever showed your father those pictures probably altered them to hide the other people. And I know exactly who it was. His sister was always furious over how he was living out his last days. She felt that he should leave his money to her. She hated me in particular because.... Joe did get attached to me. But I was pregnant. Your father was away. I guess he got very protective. He was there when you were born, Greg. I didn't get to the hospital in time.... His sister felt he was spending his money on me. God knows why. Besides, it was his money after all. So I told her off."

She looked up at each boy in turn and gave a slight smile. "I can't believe after all these years.... She must have only recently found the pictures or she would have used them before."

Germain looked uncertain. Steve, however, was relieved. He gave her a huge grin. "Ray's dad is a detective. Maybe he could look into it. Find some proof and give it to Dad."

"I don't think..." she began hesitantly.

Germain face cleared. "Yes! Let's do it," he interrupted.

"Boys, wait." Mrs. Martin took a deep breath. "Boys. Just listen for a minute." She raised her hand to halt Germain's bubble of excitement. "If you're hoping that your father and I will get back together if you find proof, forget it."

"But Mom..." Germain protested.

"No, Germain. What went on between your father and I is beyond a simple misunderstanding. If you want to find proof then find it. That's fine by me. Believe me, I would love to see the look on your father's face when he gets your proof." A twinge of bitterness had entered her voice on that last statement and Steve looked up in dismay.

She was still angry, he realized. Mr. Martin chose not to believe her and she was still mad.

She noticed his look. "I'm sorry, Greg. Maybe some years from now we'll all be able to sit and laugh this off. But not right now." She looked down at her clasped hands, then looked up again and gave them a wry smile. "I'm sorry, boys."

Steve gave her a brief reassuring nod, then looked over at Germain, who was chewing worriedly on his lips. He knew exactly what Germain was thinking. Poor Mr.

Martin. First he was wrong about Greg not being his son and now it looks as if he was also wrong about his wife cheating on him. *Yes. I'll tell Mr. Brent and ask him to help. I'm rooting for Mrs. Martin. She needs her revenge.*

It was only later, after Mrs. Martin and Germain had left, that he realized that he was thinking exactly like Greg. This was precisely what Greg would have done. Steve stared at the ceiling. *No. This is different.* They needed to find out the truth. Revenge was not his only motive. Finally, he made up his mind. He wouldn't tell Mr. Brent yet. First, he would do a bit of checking on his own. He would need more information on Joe and Joe's sister. Decision made, he picked up the phone.

Chapter Thirteen

After breaking contact with Steve, Greg wandered back to the computer monitor. He had already spent three solid hours exploring. Trying to find records on Harold Cadwell was exhausting, and so far he had turned up nothing. The doctor group that Cadwell had gone to before he died was now affiliated with a large hospital.

After a bit of checking, Greg found that the hospital kept all its medical records on a computer. Dialing into the system was a breeze. Finding the access password for vital patient information was another matter.

After a quick search on the Internet he located just the program he wanted. Best of all—it was free. He put his computer to work drumming up combinations. Half an hour later he was in. That was only the first problem: there were no records on a Harold Cadwell! More than likely the doctor had not uploaded his old records into the new system. Dead end!

Should he check other hospitals? Greg hesitated, then decided to try the closest one. Blank. There was no way he could check out every single hospital in the area. Besides, sixteen years ago most medical records were in paper files.

To ease his frustration he decided to check on Mrs. Pierce. She was busy on the phone so he decided not to disturb her. After making a small snack, Greg wandered back upstairs. As he ate, he stared in abstraction at the blank computer monitor. It was an energy-efficient monitor and Steve had set it to shut off after half an hour. He took another bite of his ham and cheese sandwich and munched slowly.

What to do? There has to be a way. Greg rubbed his temple then reached for his drink, orange juice—with pulp. *I hate pulp!* But Steve and his family obviously liked it. He took another gulp. Actually, it was beginning to grow on him. He sure didn't want to tell Steve that Mr. Pierce was his father, especially when he didn't believe it. But how was he going to prove it...?

Greg's gaze shifted to the clock. Four o'clock! He had been sitting here doing nothing for almost an hour. Mr. Pierce would soon be in. After talking to the man on the phone earlier, Greg did not look forward to seeing him any time soon.

Wait a minute! On a sudden hunch, he hurriedly put down the last uneaten bite of his sandwich, and began typing. Minutes passed as he searched through the records. It was much easier to get in the second time around. Then.... *Damn and double damn!* A grin split his jaw as he felt a rush of excitement. *Bingo! This is it! I have it.*

Greg pressed the print button. He could not believe his luck. Harold Cadwell did not have medical records on file but Daniel Pierce definitely did. Greg scrambled out of his seat, grabbing the papers as they exited the printer.

Proof! He finally had his proof! Jumping up, he ran out the door and down the stairs.

"Mom! Mom!"

Mrs. Pierce came rushing out of the kitchen. After getting in she had sent Laura home—just in case—so now she was busy preparing dinner. Her eyes were huge in panic. "Steve! My God! What's wrong?"

"I found proof! I found proof!" Greg yelled.

He grabbed her about the waist and swung her around. "I found proof, Mom."

"Steve! Steve! Put me down! What proof? Steve...."

Greg finally stood still. His face was almost splitting with his grin. "Look! Here! Read this!" He thrust the papers into her hands.

She gave him a hesitant smile then bent to read the papers. "They are results of an infertility test," she said, her voice hushed.

"Yes! Yes!" he said impatiently. "Read the results!"

She read silently, then looked up in shock. "He's infertile. It says here that he's infertile." She covered her mouth with her hands. Tears were streaming down her face. "Oh Steve! Are you sure?"

"I'm positive," Greg shouted. "And look at the date! That's before I was born. Mom, let's get out of here. Now. Before he comes in."

"Now? Steve, we can't do that. Besides it's almost...."

Greg interrupted her. "He doesn't come in until six, six-thirty. We could do it if we hurried. C'mon Mom. Let's do it." He started hurrying her toward the stairs.

"Steve, wait. I can't just leave. Steve!" she protested when he continued to push her gently in the direction of the stairs.

"Yes we can, Mom. Come on! We can leave. And now is the best time." He just felt that if he could get her out of the house now things would work out. If she stayed any longer, she would invent reasons to stay or start running scared again. He had to get her out now.

"But where will we stay?"

Greg didn't particularly care where they stayed, as long as it wasn't here. "Just pack some things and come. We can stay at a hotel for tonight. Tomorrow we can see a lawyer." He was hurrying her up the stairs as he spoke.

She was still hesitant. "Wait a minute, Steve...."

"I'll take all my school stuff." They were now at her door. "Please Mom." Greg stood, looking directly at her. "I don't want to see him beat you again. Please. This was the only reason you stayed. He can't do anything to you now. We have proof he was lying. He's infertile, so he can't be my father." She was wavering. He could see it. "Please," he pleaded, staring directly at her.

She gave a deep sigh and closed her eyes for a second. "Okay. We'll leave."

"Great! Take your credit cards. And all the cash you can. Pack your things and I'll put them in the car for you. Hurry. I'll go get mine."

He hurried. In the back of his mind was the thought that Mr. Pierce could leave work early, especially after their earlier conversation. After bringing him home, Mrs. Pierce had called her husband. Greg protested, but soon realized she was more afraid of not telling her husband the details of what had happened, only to have him find out later.

He grabbed a suitcase from the top shelf of the

closet and began pulling out drawers.

"Underwear, socks, shirts...." he was muttering under his breath as he pulled his clothes from the drawers.

All the stuff was first thrown on the bed. He then threw them haphazardly in the suitcase. Finally, he snapped the lid closed and literally ran all the way to the garage. He was breathless by the time he finished pushing it into the trunk, but he didn't stop. It was back upstairs to check on Mrs. Pierce.

< "Greg? Greg? What's wrong?">

Steve!

Greg did not want to stop to give an explanation. < "Not now. Not yet.">

< "What's happening?"> Steve was beginning to sound panicky.

< "Steve, I can't explain now. Later.">

< "No! What's wrong? Is it *him*, isn't it? Is my mother okay?">

< "She's fine. I'm fine. He's not here yet. Please Steve. I'll explain later.">

Greg sensed Steve's frustration. He ignored it and ran into Mrs. Pierce's room.

Mrs. Pierce was in a panic. She was almost blinded by tears. "I'm not sure I'm doing the right thing, Steve. Maybe we should stay and talk to him."

"No!" That was the last thing Greg wanted to do. "Did you pack?"

"I'm trying. Oh God, Steve. What if he comes in before...."

"Don't think, just pack, Mom." He grabbed one of the suitcases on the bed. "Is this ready?"

"I think so. I hope.... Oh God." She wiped at her eyes as he started for the door with the suitcase.

As he ran down the stairs, he heard a car coming up the street. He stopped dead, his heart pounding.

< "Hell, Greg!"> Steve's mental cry matched his own terror.

The car did not stop. Greg took a deep breath. He wasn't sure he was going to live through this evening. Even if they got packed, he would probably have a heart attack as soon as he reached the car.

< "Greg! I swear. If you don't tell me what's wrong...."\>

Greg knew then that he would have to give Steve some explanation. His emotions were probably driving Steve crazy. < "We're leaving him. Now. We have to pack and get out before he gets in.">

< "Leaving!">

< "Steve, please. We don't have much time. We have to get out before he gets in.">

< "But what about my mom?">

< "She agreed.">

< "What? I don't believe....">

< "Steve, I can't talk now. We have to get out.">

< "Okay. Okay. Shit! I don't know if I can live through this.">

Greg silently concurred. Another scare like that one with the car, and he knew he would be dead. He hurriedly put the suitcase in Mrs. Pierce's car, then ran back upstairs. Mrs. Pierce was almost paralyzed with fear.

She ran into his arms as he entered the door. "I heard the car."

"It was our neighbor. It passed." Greg gave her a squeeze. And it wasn't just to reassure her. He needed the body contact too. "Is the other suitcase ready?"

She pulled away slightly "I.... I think so. I...."

He went over to the suitcase. It was only half full. "Mom, it can hold some more." He went to the closet and grabbed a handful of clothing. Into the suitcase they went. Satisfied, he closed the lid and hurried away. "Come now, Mom. Just bring your bags and come now."

There was no hesitation now. She followed right behind him.

They were in the car before she spoke again. "Steve, we should leave a letter. Let him know."

Greg did not agree. "You can call him later. Or call the police and ask that they call."

She nodded then eased the car out of the garage. Suddenly she stopped. "Laura! We didn't say good bye to Laura."

Greg looked down the road. Empty. But he did not want to stop. They were just too close to escaping to chance it.

"We'll have to call her too."

Mrs. Pierce hesitated again, then nodded and started the car again.

"Where should we go?"

He didn't particularly care—anywhere but here. "Let's try a hotel first."

"Okay."

Greg collapsed back into the seat. He closed his eyes. *Damn he was tired!*

< "Steve?">

Steve answered immediately. < "I want to know everything! Everything!">

So Greg told him.

Chapter Fourteen

Complete silence.

Steve was aware that Greg was waiting for a response. In truth he couldn't give one. First he needed to control his thoughts. Jealousy! He was aware of a searing jealousy. *Mom confided in Greg. To Greg! And not to me.* He breathed slow and easy. *I have to get control or Greg will read my emotions!*

< "Steve?"> Greg was hesitant. < "I know you didn't really want.... Well I know you didn't want me to interfere but I couldn't just not do anything. It's better this way.">

< "What if he comes after her?"> Steve asked. < "Did you think of that?"> He was proud of himself. His voice didn't even sound angry.

Nevertheless Greg must still have gotten some remnants of Steve's emotions because he sounded cautious. < "I was thinking....">

Steve waited. After a pause Greg continued. < "Maybe we could get Mr. Brent to help. He's a detective, you know.">

< "I know.">

< "Well?">

< "Maybe.">

Again Greg hesitated. < "Your mom could get an order of protection so your stepfather doesn't come near her.">

< "And you think that will work?"> Steve almost snorted. < "On the news I always hear where the man kills the woman who has an order of protection.">

Steve knew Greg was definitely getting some of his anger when Greg abruptly changed the subject.

< "How is my mom?">

< "What about my mom?"> Steve was angry enough to blurt out. < "All you care about is your mom. You don't care that you're hurting my mother. You....">

< "I was trying to help your mom. She couldn't continue living with him, Steve. It was getting impossible. You know it. How can you say I don't care? If I didn't care, I wouldn't do a thing. And you know it. This entire situation....">

< "You had no right interfering,"> Steve interrupted. < "No right! I didn't mess around with your family. I did what you asked. Well that's it! You can forget about me following your advice ever again. Forget it! From now on I'll do what I want. And the first thing I'm going to do is see your father.">

< "You can't do that,"> Greg cried out.

< "Just you watch me.">

< "You… You...."> Greg was too furious to speak. < "I don't want you messing with my family. You hear me? Leave them alone!">

< "Like how you left my mother alone?">

< "What's wrong with you? I was trying to help. That's all. I wasn't trying to hurt you or anything. If you see

my father, just you wait. I'll....">

< "Go to hell! We didn't need your help!"> Steve screamed at him. Like a dam bursting its banks, his fury came bubbling over. < "You came in my family and now you've put my mom's life in danger. He's going to come after her. I know him. He's going to be furious. If he hurts her.... If my Mom gets hurt, I'll kill you. And I mean it.">

< "He was hurting her all these years....">

< "You don't know anything.">

< "I know!"> Greg stormed. < "I've being living here.">

Steve did not need the reminder. < "I wish you would get the hell out of my life. You're just messing things up. I hate you."> He sank down on the bed and abruptly cut the mental link. His eyes watered but he was determined not to cry. It was a while before he felt he was steady enough to speak without sounding weepy. Then he reached for the phone. He meant to carry out his threat. From his prior calls he had already found where Joe's sister lived.

His first call was to Germain. He needed Mr. Martin's telephone number.

Germain answered.

"Germain, it's me, Greg. I've decided to talk to Dad. Can you give me his number?"

"You're going to call him?" Germain sounded skeptical.

"Yeah."

Still Germain hesitated.

"Well? I thought you wanted me to speak to him."

"What are you going to say?"

"I'm thinking of telling him what Mom told us. You know. He could check out this Joe's sister. The whole thing sounds like one big misunderstanding. Maybe we can help."

"Alright." Germain gave him the number.

"I'll tell you how it goes," Steve promised. Immediately after hanging up he called. He did not want to get cold feet.

The phone was answered immediately.

"Hello?"

"Dad. It's Greg." Steve hoped it was indeed Mr. Martin who had answered the phone. He didn't even know his voice.

"Greg? Greg! Oh thank God. Greg!" Mr. Martin sounded almost giddy with excitement. "Listen Greg, I'm real sorry. I can't say how sorry I am. I heard that you're in the hospital again. Are you okay?"

"I'm fine Dad. Listen, can you come over? I... I.... Well... I wanted to talk to you."

"Sure I can. Give me half an hour. I'll be there. Half an hour."

"Okay."

As Mr. Martin hung up Steve slowly put down the receiver. He was doing the right thing. All along he had felt torn about what Greg wanted him to do versus what he felt was right. Although he had threatened Greg with revenge this was no act of revenge. This was right. Greg could be right where his mother was concerned but in this case Greg was wrong.

* * * *

All too soon Mr. Martin was at his room. Steve recognized him from his pictures. The older man was definitely nervous. He came slowly into the room.

"Hello, Greg." He offered a tentative smile.

"Hi." Steve was just as nervous—perhaps more so. Never in a hundred years would he have imagined himself as counselor.

Mr. Martin pulled up a chair. "Greg, I'm sorry. This mess is all my fault."

Steve definitely agreed, but it would not help if he said so. Deciding that the best policy would be to get it all out at once, he immediately launched into Mrs. Martin's story, telling Mr. Martin exactly what she had told them.

Mr. Martin spent the last few minutes of the tale with his head buried in his hands. "God!" he said, when Steve finally stopped.

"Do you believe her?" This, as far as Steve was concerned was the most important point.

Mr. Martin got up and wandered over to the window. "I wish she had told me all of this years ago."

That wasn't what Steve wanted to hear. "She tried to tell you last year but now she is mad because you didn't believe her."

"I know," he sounded weary.

"So…." Steve prompted.

Mr. Martin ran his hand through his short-cropped hair. "I don't know what to believe."

"You can believe her."

Mr. Martin looked up. He definitely recognized the ultimatum in Steve's voice. "Or I can leave, huh?"

Steve felt flushed. He looked away without

answering.

Mr. Martin came back to sit beside Steve on the bed. In a slow reflective voice he began explaining.

"Janet, Joe's sister came to my dad's office last year..." he paused. When on shore leave Mr. Martin worked as a computer consultant. The business was owned by his father.

He slowly continued. "She had a stack full of pictures, claiming them as proof that you were her nephew. Then she told me that her brother had died sixteen years ago and boxes of his belongings were stored in her basement. Because she was moving and clearing out her basement, she decided to sort out the contents of the boxes before throwing them out. She just found the pictures"

"What kind of pictures?"

"Mostly pictures of your mother and this guy Joe."

"Could the pictures be fakes?"

Mr. Martin rubbed the side of his nose. "Anything is possible. With computers..." he shrugged. "But she also had a couple of letters, which were definitely in your mother's handwriting. I really should have questioned the whole story more. But seeing those pictures, those letters.... I knew your mother must have known this guy. And she never once mentioned him. Never. I saw red. I.... I imaged your mother lying to me all these years. I guess I just blew."

"What did the letters say?"

"Nothing much. But they proved she knew him well."

"But that doesn't prove a relationship. So there! That proves it's all a fake, doesn't it?"

"Hmm."

"You don't believe her, do you?" Steve frowned at him. Mr. Martin was lounging in the chair, absently rubbing the side of his nose.

"I need to know more," he sighed. "Trust is a very delicate thing, Greg. Once the trust is gone..." again he shrugged. "Why didn't she tell me all of this sixteen years ago? My God! I am only now finding out that he was actually there when you were born. The sister told me, and now your mother has confirmed it. She never mentioned this before. All she told me is that she had to call an ambulance because you came early."

Steve said nothing. Actually, he could see Mr. Martin's point. Mrs. Martin should not have kept Joe a secret. But there was nothing they could do about that now.

"Are you going to see her and explain?"

"Does she want to see me?"

"Do you want to see her?" Steve countered. "Besides, the two of you should be discussing this. It's not fair to us, to Germain and me."

Unexpectedly, Mr. Martin grinned. "You're right. But I can't believe you're being so reasonable, Greg. I was quaking in my boots before I opened your door just now." His eyes darkened in remembered pain. "I really am sorry about what I put you through this past year. No child should have to..." He paused and looked down at his clasped hands. "Even if the entire story is true as Joe's sister said it, I should not have involved you and Germain. I shouldn't have shouted out that you weren't my son like that. I shouldn't have hit your mother. My actions... that has really bugged me these past months. My only excuse, and it's not really an excuse, is that the story festered for a good three, four hours. When I got home, I expected your mother to deny the entire thing. To have her admit it, just like that—it threw me. I'm sorry."

He should really be saying this to Greg, Steve thought with dismay. He squirmed in embarrassment.

"Okay. Okay," Mr. Martin noted his embarrassment and lifted up a reassuring hand. "Can we let bygones be bygones? Am I forgiven?"

"I guess," Steve muttered. *Now I'm really in big trouble. What's going to happen when Greg refuses to forgive and forget?*

"Good," Mr. Martin leaned over and gave him a quick hug. "I'm glad to have my son back. I promise I'll be getting more involved. I shouldn't have left your Mom, and both of you boys for long stretches like I did. By being a part-time father I messed up royally. I now see that so I've resigned from the ship; I'll be taking over my dad's business. So you may soon begin to wish I had stayed away."

Steve gave him a relieved grin. "No way!"

Mr. Martin just grinned. "I *will* try to see your mother," he continued. "I promise."

"Thanks, Dad." Steve's grin widened. He instinctively knew that until Mr. and Mrs. Martin made up, Greg would never accept his father back. "Uh... can I tell Germain everything?"

"Sure. In fact, I'll speak to him myself." He gave a frown. "You and Germain need to make up too."

Steve wasn't sure that would happen any time soon, although maybe if the parents made up, Greg and Germain might too. A sudden thought hit him. "Why did you let

Germain see you? He promised he wouldn't."

"Germain was… is going wild. Two months ago, when I got back from this last assignment, I spoke to your mother about him. We thought seeing me would help."

"Then she knows."

"That he has been seeing me?" Mr. Martin gave Steve a quizzical look. "Yes she does."

"Even late at night?" Steve tone was aggressive.

"So you found out about that night eh? We had a rare falling out that night. He came over—for no apparent reason—or rather, just to prove that he could do it." He shook his head. "In the middle of the night. I couldn't believe it when he knocked on my door. I sent him packing immediately."

They chatted for a bit more. Greg's father obviously wanted to catch up on the past year. Steve promised he would improve his grades and get back onto the honor roll. *The honor roll!* This was news to Steve. Yet he was relieved. He would no longer worry about Greg messing up his grades.

In fact, this entire evening was turning out better than he expected. He had started by trying to get back at Greg but now in a strange way he understood why Greg had tried to help his mother. He felt he had done a good deed in trying to patch up the rifts within Greg's family. From the little he had seen of Greg's father, it seemed that Greg and his father had shared a very casual and close relationship. No wonder Greg was so upset.

But Greg didn't seem to recognize how fortunate he was. Steve wished he had a father to be close to. And he was sure that Greg would not appreciate his help. In fact, he was positive that Greg wouldn't....

* * * *

After Greg's father left, Steve turned on the television for some background noise but he really wasn't watching it. What he needed to do now was make up with Greg. But how? It was a while before Steve came up with a plan.

< "Greg?" >

< "Yeah?" > Greg's reply was tentative.

< "Can you talk?" >

< "Yeah I guess. We're at a hotel. We just checked in, your Mom's in the bathroom." >

< "I think your idea about seeing Mr. Brent may work. I was thinking I could tell him you are my pen pal and I told you about him." >

Greg was silent for a minute. < "Could you call him? It would sound better coming from you." >

< "Okay. Should I call him tonight?" >

< "Call him now. Your Mom hasn't called the police yet. She is afraid to." >

< "I'll call him now then let you know how it goes, okay." >

< "Yeah," > Greg paused. < "Did you... did you see my Dad?" >

Steve was silent. Greg sounded almost apprehensive. Still, Steve hesitated. Now really was not the time to confess what he had done. Especially not now, when his motive was no longer revenge.

He had to say something. He could feel Greg's unease. < "Listen, Greg. Remember that time when we met and we talked about helping each other?">

    < "What has that got to do with anything?">

    < "Well I'm willing to agree now that your method worked with my Mom, okay.">

    < "So?">

    < "So maybe my method will work.">

    < "Your mother needed to leave your stepfather. My mom has already left my father. That's the end of it.">

    < "Your mother is unhappy and so is....">

    < "She would be worse off if she'd remained with him,"> Greg interrupted.

    < "How do you know?">

    < "I know,"> Greg insisted stubbornly.

    < "Come off it, Greg. You have no idea. You are just mad at your father, plain and simple.">

    < "You don't know anything,"> Greg burst out passionately. < "I wish we could switch back right this instant.">

    < "Well so do I, not that that's going to change anything.">

Greg blew out with noisy impatience. < "Just get in touch with Mr. Brent and let me know."> He abruptly backed out of the link.

Steve knew he was still mad. There was nothing he could do about it. He picked up the phone to call Mr. Brent.

Chapter Fifteen

Greg had a very uneasy night. Nothing would persuade Mrs. Pierce to call her husband. She was literally terrified, especially because there had been numerous attempts by her husband to contact her by phone. She had finally turned the phone off in fear of accidentally answering a call. Mr. Pierce had even called Steve's cell number. As soon as Greg heard from Steve that Mr. Brent and his brother-in-law, Mr. Connelly, were coming the next morning, he conveyed the news to Mrs. Pierce. It turned out that Mr. Connelly was a police officer.

Greg simply told Mrs. Pierce that he had a pen pal who knew some police officers. It relieved her mind somewhat. Steve also told Greg that Mr. Brent had called Mr. Pierce. This part of the news he did not tell Mrs. Pierce. She was worried enough as it was.

They were up by six and there was not much to do in the hotel suite. It was a huge room with a king-size bed, and a separate sitting area with a pullout sofa bed. Greg used the sofa bed and allowed Mrs. Pierce the privacy of the bedroom. The bathroom was enormous. Greg fully intended to take a soak in the jacuzzi before they left the hotel.

It took Greg less than half hour to get ready but Mrs. Pierce took another half-hour, so it was close to seven before they went down to the hotel restaurant. At eight, after a breakfast of toast, eggs and cereal—Mrs. Pierce had coffee only—they went back to the room to wait.

"Are you sure they're coming?" Mrs. Pierce asked for the thousandth time.

"Positive; but not before nine." He had just checked with Steve, who'd recently been discharged. Although Steve was not going to school, he still had to convince Greg's mother to let him go with Mr. Brent.

Since they had an hour to kill, he got Mrs. Pierce to call the school and make his excuses. That was no problem. They already thought he was ill from previous day. Next she spoke to Laura. Greg listened unashamedly.

It seemed that Mr. Pierce had contacted Laura when he got home and couldn't find them. Since they had packed so hurriedly he had immediately suspected what had happened.

Laura, however, was unable to give him any further information. She was not sure what he had done after she hung up with him. She only knew that he had been furious. Laura had suspected, but had been unaware of the extent of the abuse that Mrs. Pierce had been taking from Mr. Pierce. The conversation took a while and both women were teary when Mrs. Pierce finally hung up.

Once Mrs. Pierce and Greg got the newspaper they started looking at houses. They could not remain in a hotel forever. Mrs. Pierce began writing down numbers. She would start calling real estate agents as soon as the offices opened. The rest of the time was spent watching the morning news shows. Finally, just when Greg could take it no longer, there was a knock on the door.

"Oh God!" Mrs. Pierce immediately went into a panic.

Greg ran to the door. He already knew it was Steve. The mental link was stronger when they were close.

"Don't worry, it's them." He opened the door. "Hi," he greeted, a smile starting. Then he stopped abruptly, the smile frozen. His father was there.

Greg slowly moved away from the door. He gave Steve an accusing look.

< "How could you?"> he cried mentally.

Steve shrugged. < "He wanted to come.">

There was no time to say more, and Greg was so off balance by seeing his father it was a moment before he noticed that the three men were staring at him in shock. Jerkily, he moved out of the way and they all entered the room.

Then he heard Mrs. Pierce exclamation of surprise. "Are these your friends, Steve?" her voice was hesitant.

"Yes," Greg said tautly. He refused to look at Steve or greet the visitors. *I want out of here!*

Steve made the introductions.

"I need... I need to speak to my son for a second," Mrs. Pierce said. She gave the three men polite smiles then motioned to Greg. He followed her into the bedroom, eager to delay acknowledging his father.

"Steve. This is not going to work."

"Why not?" he asked impatiently.

"Steve! They are black."

Greg stared at her. Somehow he hadn't even

considered that. Neither he nor Steve had thought to mention the race of the other. "I know them," he protested.

"You know the boy," she pointed out. "But Steve we don't know how good these officers are besides... besides...."

"So because they're black you think they're no good," Greg did not hide his bitterness. The fact was, he felt betrayed. He LIKED her. And coming on top of Steve's betrayal. "Aren't you adults always telling us kids not to be prejudiced?"

She bit her lips. "I didn't mean it that way."

Totally annoyed now, and unwilling to spare her feelings, he stated flatly—"So what's the point of this conversation then?"

< "Greg?">

On hearing Steve, Greg turned away slightly, pretending to sulk.

< "What?"> his voice was short.

< "Would you believe neither Mr. Brent nor his brother-in-law want to help my mom? They don't want to get involved with a white woman's problem—a rich white woman at that. And those were their exact words."> Steve voice was definitely antagonistic. < "Didn't I tell you blacks are paranoid?">

< "Well, because they're black, your mother doesn't think they're any good."> Greg retorted.

< "Oh."> Steve was nonplussed.

< "Yeah, Oh."> Greg deliberately rubbed in his point. < "So who is paranoid now?">

< "Alright. I'll talk to them. You convince my Mom.">

Greg did not bother answering. It annoyed him

that Steve was pretending that everything was fine and that bringing his father here made no difference. He stiffened as he felt Mrs. Pierce's hand on his shoulder.

"Steve, I'm sorry. You're right."

He turned but refused to make eye contact. He was still struggling with profound feelings of hurt.

Mrs. Pierce dropped her hand, staring at him silently for a second. Quietly, she continued, "They are probably wondering what's keeping us. Let's go back."

He nodded and followed her into the room, his head down.

The conversation immediately ceased.

Greg did not bother looking up. He went over to the window and stared out.

< "Well?"> Steve asked impatiently

< "She'll let them help."> Greg could tell that Steve was still angry. More than likely because at first it seemed that the men would not help his mother. At this point he really did not care. He needed to get out for a while. As he moved towards the door, he turned to Mrs. Pierce. "I'll leave you to discuss it with them then." It was a definite challenge.

She gave him a startled look, bit her lips slightly, then gave a brief nod.

"I'll go with G... Steve," Steve started towards the door too.

Mr. Martin stood up, "I'll go out with the boys and leave you three."

"One minute, Guy," Mr. Brent called out.

Greg was already on his way out the door when Steve caught up with him.

< "Wait for me, Greg,"> Steve called mentally. As he called, he reached to halt Greg by holding on to his arm.

The contact was like an electrical charge. Both boys stood stock-still.

"Hell!" Greg cried. He blinked as page after page of his past flashed before him. *NO! Not my past! This is Steve's past!* He was in kindergarten, and then first grade.... Grade after grade, year after year! Arguing with his stepfather! Pleading with his mother!

He staggered and clutched at Steve for balance.

"Gr... Gr...," Steve gasped.

* * * *

Slowly the world straightened. Greg found himself staring at Steve. They were still clutching at each other. Anyone passing in the hallway would think they were crazy... or drunk. Steve was dead white, he looked as if he was about to faint. Greg blinked. *Steve is white!*

"I don't believe it," Greg whispered. He released Steve's shoulder to look down at his hands in wonder. He was black!

"Steve!" he cried.

Steve gasped. The shock of understanding was already in his eyes. They had changed back!

"So where do you two boys want to hang out?"

Both boys turned to stare at Mr. Martin with identical expressions of shock.

Mr. Martin gave them a puzzled look. "Are you both okay?"

Greg made a supreme effort to pull himself together. "Yes. I... Yes." He blinked a couple of times and shook his head to clear his thoughts.

"Yeah. I guess." Steve was still white. He turned to Mr. Martin. "Could we go off by ourselves to catch up? We haven't seen each other in ages."

"Sure, okay." But Mr. Martin was still mystified. He was watching them as they walked off.

"What did you think happened?" Greg asked quietly.

"Damned if I know." Steve took a deep breath.

"Well, at least we changed back."

"Yeah," Again Steve breathed in deeply.

In silence they walked to the stairs. Neither questioned the reason why they both automatically took the stairs. They needed privacy and they needed to sit. Both were still shaky.

Greg opened the heavy fireproof door of the stairwell. They sat on the first step, backs to the wall.

"Can you still read my mind?" Steve asked after a long moment of silence.

Greg leaned back, his head against the wall, and tried. Steve's thoughts were crystal clear. "Yeah. What happens now?" he asked. Then, "Never mind."

Steve rubbed the side of his face in exasperation. Greg grinned, slowly. It was impossible for Steve to hide his thoughts. And Steve wanted him and his father to make up. In fact, he already knew exactly what had happened.

"I'll try." He answered the unasked question.

Steve nodded. He too was getting Greg's thoughts, so he knew that Greg truly meant what he said. "The touching did it. If I had known that before I would have squeezed you to death days ago."

Greg just grinned. The touching had changed them both, perhaps irreversibly. They were now almost as one. In those few seconds he had practically lived Steve's life and he knew that the same thing had happened to Steve. What Steve had experienced he had experienced and vice versa. He remembered parts of a poem he had once heard long ago, about only knowing someone after walking in their footsteps. He had literally done just that with Steve.

* * * *

"Let's go back," Steve stood. They had needed time to recover from the shock of the switch. They did not need time to discuss their different situations. That they already knew.

Six Months Later

Mr. Pierce was never charged with a crime. Despite Steve's pleading and the pleading of both Mr. Brent and Mr. Connelly, his mother refused to charge Mr. Pierce because of fear of the publicity. Her other reason was that Greg's method of getting the medical information was not legal. She thought that Steve would get into trouble if there was a public trial.

In fact, Steve ended up getting a blistering warning about computer hacking from Mr. Brent. He in turn was furious with Greg, since he could hardly point out that it was Greg and not him who had hacked into the hospital's computer—and Greg's snickers did nothing to soothe his anger.

Although Steve was sorry that his stepfather would not pay for all the years of abusing his mother, he was not sorry to have escaped the publicity of a trial. And since neither Mr. Brent nor Mr. Connelly wanted his mother hurt, they made sure to enlist all their fellow police officers to keep tabs on Mr. Pierce. Steve was just glad that Mr. Pierce was aware that the police were keeping an eye on him, his activity, plus watching out for Steve's mom. Better yet, after a deliberately planned campaign of repeated harassment and confrontations with the police, Mr. Pierce was forced to move away. He was now living in Connecticut. Steve and Greg speculated that some of the adults' actions weren't totally legal but they weren't going to complain. His mom and Mr. Pierce were getting a divorce and had sold the house. Also, with encouragement from Mrs. Martin, his mom had decided that she needed therapy to restore her self confidence. Steve was pleased. He knew that his mom had paid a heavy emotional price for the years of abuse. He wanted her happy again.

Steve knew in his bones that he and Greg would be linked for life. They were now fast friends and often slept over at each other's home even though they were constantly bickering and accusing each other of invading the other's privacy. The fact is, they were both worried about privacy—about future dating—and worked hard to cultivate mental blocks. That worked only to some extent. If they were miles apart, keeping secrets from each other wasn't too hard. However, when together the only way to maintain privacy was to set fixed, unbreakable rules. They both agreed to block each other's thoughts. It was a constant mental battle that was fortunately getting easier.

Steve liked Mr. Martin and eagerly began using him as a father-figure. He was especially happy when Mr. Martin moved back home. For a while it was touch-and-go, but with Mr. Brent's help, they were able to prove Mrs. Martin's version of events. Also, Mrs. Martin actually admitted that she was wrong to hide the truth from her husband for all these years. In fact, she had feared that his jealousy would lead to the exact misunderstanding that had occurred. All was not yet perfect—but they were working on it and both Mr. and Mrs. Martin had decided to try to save their marriage. They went through some intense counseling before getting back together. Even Germain settled down. He was forced to—what with Mr. Martin now a fulltime father.

School was another story. Steve's mom liked the school system and did not want to further disrupt his life so she bought another house in the same school district—that was her story. His take on it was that she liked the school system, period, so he still had Tony to deal with. He was unable to squash the Forever Against Tony or F.A.T. group that formed. The group was growing in leaps and bounds, and since Tony was never going to forgive him, he decided to join. Maybe he could influence them a bit so they didn't go overboard with this hate thing. At Greg's school, Steve tried to encourage Greg to confront the teachers about the separation of the races. Greg, while recognizing that his school had racial issues, initially refused to go along with Steve's plan. However, during a visit by Steve to the school, they both approached the principal. To Steve's surprise the principal was very receptive. Ten kids, including Greg and Ray, were selected for a peer training group. The plan was to give focused skits and lectures to small groups of students and to look out for any opportunity that would bring groups together. Since it was sponsored by the principal even teachers were getting involved.

Ray became the only person to be included in their big secret. The three of them got together whenever Steve came back to Greg's school. Steve liked Ray and did not want to lose him as a friend. After hearing from Greg how confused Ray was, they decided to swear him to secrecy and tell him about their mental link. Imagine his shock and disbelief! Anyway, after they both backed away—in horror!—from Ray's wild proposals to use their mental link to have fun with others, Ray told them they were both tame and moved on. Fortunately, Ray was soon too happy to care. On a two-day visit to Steve's school, Ray met his first girlfriend. He came back bubbling over in excitement and although Greg and Steve ragged him for days he stuck it out. He was now seeing the girl on a regular basis.

It was not all easy; every now and again they would slip up. In fact, Steve was sure that his mother suspected something. And Mr. and Mrs. Martin were always giving them strange looks. Maybe one day soon they would tell the adults exactly what was going on. Right now they were experimenting....

Wouldn't it be great to switch back and forth at will?

The End

Thank you for reading *Linked* by Olive Peart

Author's Bio

Olive Peart has navigated different urban and suburban school systems with her three children and *Linked* reflects what she has seen, heard and experienced over the years. She is an accomplished author and educator in her primary profession of radiography, which she both practices and teaches. She regularly writes articles for radiological journals and newsmagazines and gives lectures on radiography related topics at seminars across the United States. Her other published books–all health care related–include: *Spanish for Professionals in Radiology*; *Lange Q & A Mammography Examination*; and *Mammography and Breast Imaging-Just the Facts*. When not writing, Olive is often occupied with her other addiction—reading. Born on the beautiful Caribbean island of Jamaica, she lives with her husband and children in the Northeast. Olive loves to hear from her readers, and may be reached at www.opeart.com by email: olive@opeart.com